Twelve Stories for Fall

D0735923

Twelve Stories for Fall

Linda Mansfield

A Restart Communications, LLC publication

Dedication

To the people who have been most helpful in my fiction-writing adventure to date:

For their continuous encouragement: Anita Millican, Nena Ray, Marti Humphrey, James Knapp, Glenda Lacer, Barbara Ragonese, Andy Lally, Rick Maas, Brad King, Amy Hall and Camas Breen-Brandt.

My beta readers: Nena Ray and Anita Millican.

Craft-show merchandiser extraordinaire: Wanda Devin.

The person who bought the first copy of my first book: The late Dennis Hunley.

Friends who bought oodles of copies for Christmas gifts: Marti Humphrey, Geoff Dodge, Gene Nolen, John Heydenreich, Anita Millican, the late Joan Norris, Ray and Brenda Quinn, Nena Ray.

The reviewers; you know who you are. Thank you!

Companies that helped: Pressbooks, Lulu, Dominion

Editorial, Barnes & Noble (especially the Plainfield, Ind., store and the Barnes & Noble River Crossing in Indianapolis), Bookmamas, Frazee Gardens, Indy Reads Books, Three Sisters and a Trunk, The Vault, Amazon, IngramSpark, Smashwords, Books Go Social.

Other entities that helped: The Geeky Press, Indianapolis Public Library, Junior League of Indianapolis, North United Methodist Church, The Indiana Historical Society, The Greenwood (Ind.) Public Library, Writer's Center of Indiana, Arthur M. Glick JCC Indianapolis, Indianapolis chapter of the National League of American Pen Women.

And last but certainly not least, members of the press for getting the word out!

Contents

Reviews

**WHAT THEY'RE SAYING ABOUT
"STORIES FOR THE 12 DAYS OF CHRISTMAS"**

"If you travel a lot, do your nerves a favor; get this book!" — *Kathryn,
an Amazon reviewer*

"Stories for the 12 Days of Christmas" is a little like grabbing a
cookie or two at a time." — *Susan Schoch, Story Circle Book Reviews*

**WHAT THEY'RE SAYING ABOUT "TWELVE
STORIES FOR SPRING"**

"I could not stop reading until the very end!" — *Anita Millican*

"Buy this book…now!" — *An Amazon customer*

**WHAT THEY'RE SAYING ABOUT "TWELVE
STORIES FOR SUMMER"**

"Part of the reason I love your books is they're a relaxing, easy read."
— *Brenda Labos via Twitter*

Introduction

Indianapolis, Ind.

I love fall.

The primary reason is the fall foliage. Nature goes all out to celebrate the harvest and give us something nice to remember during the gloomy, cold days of winter. Fall's changing leaves in brilliant shades of gold, scarlet, cranberry and orange along with the season's crisp air can rejuvenate a person after the heat and humidity of summer. Mix in some pumpkins, apple cider, cinnamon candles, tailgating at football games and of course Halloween, and autumn is spectacular.

In my previous three collections of short stories in the "Two Good Feet" series — "Stories for the 12 Days of Christmas," "Twelve Stories for Spring" and "Twelve Stories for Summer" — I tried to make my fiction as realistic as possible.

That plan went out the window with "Twelve Stories for Fall."

I primarily make my living as a motorsports public relations person. One of my racing friends, Don Kay, hosts a live racing interview show every Tuesday at 7 p.m. at a pub in Speedway, Indiana called McGilvery's. (See AutosportRadio.com. If you can't be there in person you can watch the live stream on YouTube through a link on that Web site, or you can catch the shows later on YouTube. At press time Don was planning to start streaming the shows live on Facebook and Twitter too.)

Don interviews people from various forms of motorsports, but the show has a definite IndyCar theme. The Indianapolis Motor Speedway is a couple of miles away and the show is sponsored in part by Honda, Honda HPD, the Indianapolis Motor Speedway and the Verizon IndyCar Series. Think of it kind of like "Cheers" where most of the patrons love the smell of burning rubber. I'd say it's "where everybody knows your name" too, except I attend often and I'm terrible with names.

Don has been nice enough to have me as a guest on his show a couple of times. In 2015 he talked to me on the air about my first book. During the interview I told him of my plans to continue the Christmas book through three more books centered on spring, summer and fall. He planted an idea in my mind during the interview when he mentioned he liked mysteries and said it would be nice if the fall book had some stories of that genre.

I'm not into the vampires, werewolves and the like that are popular today, but I enjoy a good mystery too. After writing a couple of stories for "Twelve Stories for Fall," I thought *What the heck! I'll take Don's suggestion and see if I can write a couple of mysteries for this one.*

The first two stories and the last one in this book aren't mysteries. I was toying with the idea when I wrote the first two stories, and the last story didn't lend itself to that treatment. But in stories three through 12 I somehow ended up with some bats, an arsonist, two kidnappers, a couple of detectives, a couple of guns, three murderers, a horse thief, a skeleton, a snake, and six ghosts. (I was as surprised as anybody!)

The goal for my first three collections of fictional short stories was to provide entertaining, quick reads for teenagers through senior citizens, male and female. This book's goal is the same, and I'd love to know what you think. You can reach me through my Web site (LindaMansfieldBooks.com), Facebook (Linda Mansfield — Author) or Twitter (@RestartLMAuthor). If you are kind enough to join my mailing list through the form on the home page of my Web site, I'll e-mail you a free short story as my thank you. I won't sell your e-mail address, and you can unsubscribe anytime. I also won't flood you with messages.

And as always, if you enjoyed this book, I'd appreciate you posting a short review at the outlet where you obtained it. The number of reviews an author has contributes to how much attention these companies give to authors, so each review is important and appreciated.

Happy fall!
Linda Mansfield

1

It Takes a Village

Kathy Simpson smashed her yellow smock onto its hook in her locker, snatched her purse and jacket, slammed the locker door shut, and hurried out the back door of the dollar store, slamming it too. She didn't notice the crisp air that Friday evening in early October because she was holding her breath, trying hard not to cry until she was inside her car. Feelings of shock, manipulation, anger, and frustration collided as she reacted to the news her long-missing ex-husband was getting the job she wanted, and he was going to be her new boss starting on Monday.

The dollar store had been without a manager for two months. Kathy had been a cashier there since opening day six years ago, and she was due for a raise. She had expressed interest in the manager position, and she thought she was in the running for it. But corporate was sending someone with a college education to fill the opening and that person was Bobby Simpson, the father of her only son.

Her heart wondered how she was going to work under a man who had caused her so much pain. Her more practical head pointed out now he had a job, perhaps he could catch up with his child-support payments.

Her son, Luke, had just started fifth grade. He'd be delighted his happy-go-lucky dad was back in the picture, but this time Kathy would set better boundaries because problems invariably followed Bobby Simpson wherever he went.

She said nothing about it when she got home. Her mother had prepared Luke's supper and helped him finish his homework, on schedule. It was one of the house rules that the weekend's homework would be completed each Friday night before the allure of the weekend caused any procrastination.

"Are you OK?" her mother asked her when she arrived home.

"I'm fine; thanks," Kathy replied. There would be plenty of time to fill her mom in later, after she wrapped her head around the news herself.

The letter arrived in Saturday morning's mail. The return address showed it was from a Catholic church in Arkansas. Kathy didn't know a soul in Arkansas. She sat at the kitchen table, tore the envelope open, and gained more insight.

Dear Kathy,

We've never met, but I've been helping Bobby Simpson for the last several months as he recuperated from injuries he sustained helping a young robbery victim.

When I met him, Bobby seemed to be lost. He has made many steps to improve his situation since I've known him, and he wants to resume his responsibilities as a father.

There were few job openings in your area, but he has found a position at the store where you work. I hope you will not take this as a form of encroachment on your own position there, but will instead give him the benefit of the doubt as he tries to improve his life, be near his son, and help support him.

At least at first, he will be living at the volunteer fire department in exchange for part-time work there.

Bobby told me you think he's a bad person. If he ever was, I assure you he's changed. He responded admirably in the robbery he encountered, and required hospitalization following his role as a Good Samaritan. He has made mistakes, but I believe he is a good man.

If I can be of any help, please call me at the number on this stationery's letterhead. Meanwhile, I will continue to hold all of you in my prayers.

Sincerely,

Father Peter Francis McCarthy

Hmm Kathy thought. *He's had his teacher send a note home.*

But she thought about the priest's words periodically the rest of the weekend, and she slid the note in a dresser drawer for safekeeping.

As she predicted, Luke was happy when she told him his dad would soon be back in town. Her mother's reaction was one of concern, like her own.

I have to remain professional at all times, Kathy told herself one more time on Monday afternoon when she entered the back of the dollar store. She stowed her pocketbook and jacket in her locker, put on the yellow smock hanging there, and steeled herself for what lay ahead.

Bobby was in the tiny office a few feet away. She could see the back of his head, covered with long, thick, blond hair. He was turned at an angle as he rummaged through a putty-colored vertical file cabinet, but he lowered the folders he had in his hands as he saw her draw abreast of the door.

"It's good to see you, Kathy," he murmured, looking at her with the deep blue eyes that had been her downfall many times.

The time clock in the hallway next to the door clicked loudly. Kathy reached for her card and punched in, and then turned to the man who could still take her breath away no matter how hard she tried to deny it.

"Hello, Bobby," she said stiffly as she continued down the hall. "Congratulations on your new job."

They avoided each other the rest of her shift.

As she was clocking out, Kathy got the question she knew was coming.

"When can I see Luke?"

Legally she didn't have to let him have any contact. Luke wanted his father in his life, however, and Kathy knew it would be impossible to keep them apart in such a small town.

Her answer was well prepared. "You can take him to and from football practice on Saturday mornings if you like," she said flatly. "You can pick him up at 8:15 and drop him off at 11 at The Brown Jug. I'll be there until the lunch shift is over."

It was all polite.

Bobby took a deep breath. "Are you ever going to forgive me?"

Kathy refused to look into his piercing, sapphire-blue eyes. It had been a question, not a real apology. "I will not discuss this at work" she said firmly, and marched out the door.

Bobby's first check for child support arrived in the mail three days after payday. The pair continued to tiptoe around each other at the store in the ensuing days, like wild animals avoiding an adversary.

It was easy to get the latest gossip in a town as small as Mainsville. It didn't take Bobby long to learn Kathy was seeing a new guy at the power plant named Dave Something-or-the-other. She didn't have much time for a social life and no one thought it was serious yet, but everyone in town knew they had become friends.

Kathy continued to allow Bobby to do some car-pooling. His next run would be late Saturday afternoon, when Luke was invited to a bonfire at 6 p.m. at Hemlock State Park outside of town. It was a get-together for a bunch of kids who had taken swimming lessons there over the summer.

Kathy had to admit so far Bobby had been punctual. He picked up Luke at 5:30.

She got the call that stabbed fear into her soul around 8.

It was from Ron Martin, the park's only ranger. The kids had gone on a scavenger hunt, and all of them except Luke had returned more than an hour ago.

"I'll be right there," she said breathlessly.

Ron also called the local police and the fire department. Kathy wasn't sure if she was fit to drive, so she called her friend, Dave Shepherd, who dropped everything to come get her and take her to the park. He didn't take time to get a babysitter so his daughter, Jill, was in the back seat of his SUV.

By the time they pulled into the same parking lot where they'd met in July, about two dozen people were already combing the trails for Luke. The smell of pine trees permeated the area, and a large harvest moon rose over the mountains.

"He can't be far," Dave told Kathy as he prepared to join the search. "Stay at the bonfire with Jill, and call me if he shows up."

Something made Dave take the left route to the circular trail nearest the kids' campfire, while everyone else had taken the right.

Less than 10 minutes up the small mountain path, Dave found it covered with shale from a small avalanche.

"Luke?" he called out in the darkness while shining his flashlight around.

"I'm here, Dave!" Luke was standing on a small ledge about 20 feet under the edge of the trail, where he'd fallen when the ground gave way.

"Are you hurt?" Dave asked.

"I'm bleeding a little bit, but not too bad," Luke said bravely. "Can you come get me?"

"I'll be right there, but let me call your mom first," Dave said. He was thankful to see he had cell-phone service. Kathy picked up immediately and was relieved to hear Luke was OK. He told her where they were, and told her to call the leaders of the other search parties.

Knowing more help was on the way, Dave slid down the hill as if he'd been an experienced hiker. Luke didn't have any broken bones, but he had a few cuts and bruises.

About 15 minutes later the cavalry arrived.

Bobby, who had been playing pool at the fire hall when the initial call came in, was among the first firefighters to reach Dave and Luke. He threw a long rope to Dave, and Dave knotted it around the boy. Bobby, several other firefighters, and one of the strongest men in the area, Big Al from Al's Towing, held tight to the rope and slowly pulled Luke up. After he was back on the trail, they repeated the process with Dave.

When they arrived back at the bonfire, the firefighters patched Luke's cuts up with ointment and bandages after they pried him from his mother's embrace.

Only when it was over did Bobby react. He bent, touched his son's right shoulder with one hand, and looked into blue eyes so like his own. "I don't know what I would have done if you'd been hurt," he said, and then quickly stood and looked into Kathy's eyes. She returned his gaze, but when she suddenly thought he might kiss her, she looked away. Her ex-husband could still conjure up a lot of emotions, even with their history and the fact he was now her boss. She almost wished he'd stayed missing, except for his child-support payments and the fact Luke adored him. She had to admit she appreciated his help with Luke too.

"Can we have pizza back at The Brown Jug?" Luke asked, oblivious to his parents. "I'm kind of hungry!"

Later, before Kathy, Luke, Dave, Jill, Bobby, and Kathy's mother shared three large pepperoni pies, Kathy said a silent prayer of gratitude that her son was safe. She looked around the table at her family and friends and thought about how many people had dropped everything to help.

"I guess it does take a village to raise a child," she said softly.

2

Doing All You Can

Roger Markowitz took a deep breath, applied a smile, and opened the door to Room 227 of Broward Health Medical Center.

His father looked up at him from his hospital bed. Perhaps he was surprised. Maybe he was annoyed. Roger didn't know which emotion was accurate, but he'd never been good at reading his father.

A small television hanging from the ceiling parallel to the foot of the bed was tuned to a sports channel. Two commentators squawked about the performances they'd seen during yesterday's football games.

Amos snapped the TV off with a remote control resting under his right hand.

A welcome would have been too hard. "Why did you come? I'm OK," he barked, running the fingers of his left hand through his wavy, steel-gray hair. It was remarkably thick for a man of 79.

Roger followed his usual pattern and ignored the comment. He couldn't remember a time when he pleased his father. One more jab didn't matter. He hadn't flown all the way from Manhattan to Florida that Monday morning in October to fight. "How are you feeling?" he asked, taking the high road.

"Like shit," Amos replied, moving his head in a small circle. "How do you think you feel after open-heart surgery?"

"I'm sure it's difficult," Roger said, determined not to let his father get the best of him. "Mom says the doctors say you're doing well, though."

Amos grunted in response, unwilling for any optimism.

Roger looked at the clock on the wall. It was 3 p.m. He hadn't been in the room five minutes, but it felt like five hours.

"Where's Mom?" he asked.

"I don't know; she was here, but I must have fallen asleep," his father said. "Did you fly in this morning?"

"Yes."

"Well, you needn't have spent the money. I'm fine."

"I used frequent-flyer miles," Roger said to please him, but immediately regretted it. His father would have been more impressed if he'd paid through the nose. It always was 'damned if you do, damned if you don't' where his father was concerned. Amos's current condition hadn't changed anything.

Both men looked relieved when Roger's mother, Lavana, opened the door and breezed into the room. She was as short as her son and husband were tall. She still dyed her hair the auburn it was in her youth. The only concessions she'd made to getting older were her dentures and the pair of dark brown, plastic reading glasses perched on the top of her head.

"Why, Roger! How nice! When did you get here?" she chirped as she looked up at her only child, now a grown man with a responsible job in Manhattan.

"A few minutes ago," Roger said. "Dad looks good!"

"Don't talk like I'm not in the room," Amos snarled.

"Yes, the doctor said everything went well" Lavana agreed, ignoring him. "He has to blow into this apparatus now, to clear his lungs so he doesn't get pneumonia, but it hurts."

The blue and clear-plastic contraption was on a portable table above the bed. Lavana pushed it closer to her husband. With a frown and a wince he picked the apparatus up and dutifully blew into it. Four blue plastic balls rose about halfway up the clear-plastic cylinders encasing them.

"Good! Try again," she encouraged with the enthusiasm of an elementary schoolteacher.

Lavana had been dealing with her husband and running interference between him and their son for a long time. For a couple of years, Roger had kept contact only through phone calls. She was encouraged when Roger visited them for a few days last January at the end of a holiday trip to Cancun.

It had been at least 15 minutes since his arrival, so Roger felt he deserved a break.

"I didn't have lunch, so I'm going to go to the cafeteria," he said. "Do either of you need anything?"

"A strawberry milkshake with lots of whipped cream," his father said sarcastically.

"You go, dear," his mother said.

Roger headed to the cafeteria, where he ate an institutionalized chicken salad sandwich and some chips, washed them down with a soft drink, and wondered if there was some way to connect with his father.

They didn't have much in common except for some genes.

And our gene pool could have used some chlorine somewhere along the way, Roger joked to himself.

He bought a strawberry milkshake for Amos before he left the cafeteria, and headed for the elevator.

A pleasant but tired RN gave him the once-over as he passed the nurse's station near his father's room.

"Are you Amos Markowitz's son?" she guessed, looking up from a computer.

"Guilty as charged," he replied.

"Well, I'm his day nurse, Maggie Jones," she said. "He's doing well, considering. I just wanted to mention that family members often give blood while they're here because our blood bank's supplies are low. If you'd like to contribute, here's the information," she said, handing him a blue sheet of paper.

"Thank you; I will," Roger replied.

His mother met him inside the door to his father's room, and gave him a quick hug.

"He dropped off to sleep, so let's go into the waiting room," she whispered. Roger put the milkshake and a napkin on the rolling table and followed his mother down the hall.

"Like I told you on the phone, he had a heart attack on the golf course on Saturday," she said, sinking into a modern, orange vinyl chair as her words rushed out. "He was arguing with Tony Baldwin about how to take some shot, and he collapsed. Luckily they all had cell phones. Tony gave him CPR. The ambulance came quickly and drove right onto the golf course. The doctor who operated on him said two arteries were blocked; one about 60 percent and the other completely."

"And how are you holding up, Mom?" Roger asked.

"Oh, I'm fine," she said, dismissing any thought of herself. "But I don't know how I'm going to get him to listen to the doctors. He has never been good at that."

"He's never been good at listening to anything that wasn't what he wanted to hear," Roger noted.

"Well, yes, there's that too," his mother admitted.

Amos was awake and finishing the milkshake when they returned to his room. He made a slurping sound as he dragged the last bit of milkshake through his straw.

"That tasted good," he admitted.

Maggie, his nurse, stepped briskly into the room and checked his blood pressure.

"Who gave you a milkshake?" she demanded.

"It hit the spot," Amos told her.

"Well, your blood pressure went sky high," she responded, shaking her head.

For the next two days, Lavana and Roger stood guard over Amos, responding to his requests and listening to his complaints. Roger donated blood, got caught up on some reading on his iPad, and stayed out of the way as much as possible.

After they left the hospital at the end of the visiting hours, Roger slept on a pullout couch in the living room of Amos and Lavana's condo. Their apartment was on the second floor of an eight-story building, but it faced the ocean and Roger enjoyed the sound of the waves hitting the shore before he drifted off to sleep. It did seem strange to be at the beach in October though.

Before he went to bed that first night, Roger pulled open a sliding door in the living room and stepped onto a small balcony facing the ocean. The waves were dark, but he could see the white foam as it hit the beach. A new moon made promises to anyone who believed it could, while a brightly lit casino boat partied its way south. It was a strange piece of human society amidst the natural ocean view.

Unless he was spending a weekend at the cabin he rented in the

Hamptons, Roger almost forgot he lived a few miles from this same ocean. The view from the balcony of his apartment in Manhattan was of the Empire State Building. The only time Roger remembered he lived on an island was when he waited in traffic to cross a bridge.

Roger took a deep breath of the salty air. The ocean itself didn't look any different to the casual passerby, but the air was a little crisper, signifying a change in the seasons. It was as if the beach itself had said goodbye to the sun worshipers and the smell of suntan lotion in the summer, and was taking its own deep breath before the snowbirds descended over the winter.

On the morning of the third day, while he and his mother were eating cinnamon bagels with a cream-cheese schmear for breakfast before they left for the hospital, Roger asked the questions his sense of duty demanded he ask.

"How will you cope when Dad gets out of the hospital? Will you have enough help? Do you need any money?"

"I'll be fine, dear," his mother assured him. "We'll take a cab to the doctor's appointments, and everyone in our card club said they'd help. We'll be fine."

"You can't lift him, you know," he pointed out. "I'll be glad to pay for some help until he's better."

"Let me give it a try myself first. If I need help, I promise to let you know and we'll have someone come in," Lavana agreed.

"Promise?" her son prodded.

"Promise."

Later that afternoon, Roger was sitting in an armchair by his father's bed, reading the latest copy of "Forbes" on his iPad. He usually enjoyed the daily quotations the magazine presented, but he didn't understand today's quote. It was by the Scottish philosopher

Thomas Carlyle, who wrote, "Men do less than they ought, unless they do all that they can."

He was still thinking about the quote when Tony popped his head inside the door.

"How are you doing, old man?" Tony asked Amos. "You didn't have to have a heart attack because I was beating you, you know."

"I was right about that shot!" Amos snarled, but he was pleased to see his friend. The pair had worked together years ago in Brooklyn, and Tony and his wife had followed Roger's parents to Fort Lauderdale a couple of years after he retired.

"Roger! It's great to see you!" Tony said when he spotted him. "I haven't seen you since, well, I don't know when I last saw you!"

"It's nice to see you again, Mr. Baldwin," Roger said. Although they were all adults now, some habits were hard to break.

"Your dad keeps me up to date on what you're doing," Tony said, ignoring the look of absolute pain that crossed Amos's face at the words.

"Really?" Roger asked.

"Really," Tony confirmed.

"Hey, Baldwin, when are you going to sell me your old golf cart?" Amos said, changing the subject like a kid who realized he'd been caught in a lie.

Maybe my old man doesn't hate me as much as he lets on, Roger thought as the conversation switched to the latest woes of the Jets and the Giants. When they launched into politics, Roger gave up and said his goodbyes.

Amos was discharged from the hospital the following morning. Lavana pushed the obligatory wheelchair on the ride to Roger's rental car, and the short trip to the condo was uneventful. Lavana and Amos disagreed about which pharmacy to use to fill Amos's new prescriptions, but Amos won, and Roger filled them later that afternoon. He was scheduled to fly back to New York on a 7 p.m. flight.

His mother kissed him goodbye on the cheek when it was time for him to leave for the airport, and thanked him for coming.

"Have a good trip home," Amos said because he felt obligated to say something. "You'll have to come back another time to get your inheritance," he added.

Roger smiled. "OK, Dad," he agreed as he carried his suitcase out the condo door.

3

The Case of the Lime-Green Lighter

A thunderstorm was imminent as Matt Stine hurried to let the steers into his grandmother's barn that October afternoon. His ball game after school had already been canceled due to the forecast, and dry leaves whipped in the stiff wind preceding the storm. Several bats flew in and out of a small window near the peak of the roof of the old gray wooden barn. An unseen rat scurried along the wall as Matt slid the heavy barn door closed. He didn't mind giving his grandmother a hand, but being close to where his grandfather died gave him the creeps.

The coroner had ruled Sam Stine died of a heart attack while battling a hay fire caused by bales that were too dry when they were formed. The county agent said bacteria had made them burn. It was possible his grandfather may have made a deadly mistake when he baled them one morning when the humidity was high. But Sam had been a farmer all his life, and Matt couldn't help thinking there was more to the story.

Matt's grandmother, Bernice Stine, had just gotten home from her beauty shop that tragic day and was thinking about what to make for supper when she saw the flames. She dialed 9-1-1, and the Chapel Hill Volunteer Fire Company saved most of the barn and all the livestock. But when they arrived Bernice was cradling the limp body of her husband of 40 years in her arms. There was nothing that could be done to save him.

The fire made all the local news outlets, and there was a huge turnout at Sam's viewing and funeral. It made it even harder for Matt to come up with a motive if foul play had been involved, because as far as he knew his grandfather had no enemies.

Most of the townspeople accepted the theory that Sam had a heart attack while fighting the fire. The tragedy was a primary topic of conversation until another unfortunate fire occurred several months later at the Christmas Eve service at the Baptist church, but luckily no one had been injured in that one.

A bolt of lightning cracked the sky and interrupted Matt's thoughts. Large raindrops slid at an angle in the wind as they pelted his young, athletic body. He started to run inside but stopped abruptly when he spied a lime-green Bic lighter partly buried in the dirt. Pushing his long brown hair out of his eyes with one hand, Matt used the other to pry the lighter out of the brown dirt that was on its way to becoming mud. He dropped the lighter into the right-front pocket of his jeans before dashing to the house, but he didn't tell his grandmother anything about his discovery. If he had, she would have been quick to confirm no one on the farm smoked.

The next afternoon, right after school, Matt dropped the lighter onto the calendar desk blotter on Detective Myers' scarred, old wooden desk at the police station. He and Detective Myers kept their theories close to their vests, but they both had a hunch Sam's fire and heart attack weren't necessarily natural. They were also the only ones in town who knew aviation fuel had been found at the site of the fire during the initial investigation last year.

That's about all they had, though. The farm was located at the end of a long dirt driveway off a rural road, and despite questioning many neighbors, no one could remember seeing anyone unusual the day of the fire. No vehicle tire tracks were found other than those of the family car and Sam's pickup. A couple of small tracks were discovered near the edge of the barnyard, but they were from the tread of the tires on Sam's own John Deere tractor.

"I found it in the barnyard," Matt told the heavy-set detective, who pushed aside a ham sub sandwich and its wrapper to examine the lighter.

"Hmm," was all Detective Myers said at first as he wiped his hands on his dark brown pants. "So much time has passed I doubt if we'll find anything on it, but I'll send it to the lab," he said a few heartbeats later.

"Is there anything new in the case?" Matt asked.

"Well, an arsonist was caught in Monroe County last week; he was setting fire to a dumpster behind an apartment complex," Detective Myers said. "I'm driving up there tomorrow to talk to him, and to see if I can place him here around the time of your grand-dad's fire. So far they say he hasn't been cooperative. He doesn't say much, and he seems to be a drifter. Nobody has pried much out of him yet."

"OK; keep me posted," Matt said.

"And you keep doing what you've been doing," Detective Myers answered. "If you find anything else, or see or hear anything, let me know."

"You bet," Matt replied as he rose to leave.

Detective Myers' interview of the suspect the following day didn't reveal anything new, as he was uncooperative. When he was first brought in, he admitted to setting one fire as a teen, but then he clammed up. No prior incidents had shown up in the records, but that county's sheriff was checking to see if his suspect went by any aliases. In the meantime, Detective Myers had found his name in the computerized lists of guests at the Days Inn one town over the night before the Stine fire, so both he and Matt thought they might be on to something.

Meanwhile, life in Chapel Hill continued like it always did.

The elementary and junior-high kids were all happily anticipating the town's Halloween parade and trick or treating, while the high-school kids like Matt were looking forward to the annual bonfire and big football game against Maple Grove High. Matt was taking Marti Cook to both.

The bonfire was held at Chapel Hill Park. Along with the usual high-school kids, it attracted a few adults, including those who normally spent their evenings in the local bars. Some considered the bonfire an even better opportunity to drink than the football game itself.

The bonfire was in full swing when Matt and Marti found a place on a bench made from a wooden plank resting on some hay bales. They hadn't been sure what to wear to be warm enough, but their jeans, white shirts under bulky sweaters, and boots fit the bill. Matt's sweater was dark green, while Marti's was rust. She had added a matching hat, and they both looked great as they chatted on the makeshift bench.

Marti had brought along a thermos filled with hot cider. They shared the spicy beverage as they watched the orange and yellow flames from the bonfire shoot towards the sky. The logs crackled and snapped like teachers drawing their classes to attention. The air was crisp, and a large yellow moon rose in the sky. The unmistakable sights, sounds, and smells of autumn were like nature itself was celebrating all the harvest had supplied in preparation for the upcoming hard winter.

Two old men who had a head start on their drinking were sitting on a plank right in front of Matt and Marti. Matt had seen them both before, but he didn't know either. They hung out at the VFW, but they usually showed up at his church at Christmas. They weren't drunk, but they were on their way. Matt and Marti couldn't help but overhear the two men as they commiserated over years past.

Matt was about to suggest to Marti that they move when he overheard something that made the hairs on the back of his neck stand straight up.

"This isn't anywhere near as good as my fire at the old Stine place," one of the old men bragged to the other as he lit the stump of a cigar with a lime-green Bic lighter. "That one was four times the size of this one."

Matt's eyes grew as wide as the full moon.

"Did you hear that?" he whispered to Marti.

"Yes!"

"We have to get Detective Myers right away," Matt said softly but firmly.

Matt looked around for a police officer, but they were all directing traffic and parking cars.

"Come on, Marti!" he urged. "We need to get to the police station right away!"

Unfortunately, the men hadn't been drinking as long as Matt

thought they had. The bigger man turned towards them in recognition and sneered.

"You're one of Sam Stine's grandkids, aren't you?" he asked.

Matt didn't reply. He grabbed Marti's hand, and they hurried to Matt's old Mustang in the parking lot. But the man was right behind them, and he took a swing at Matt as Matt was unlocking the driver's side door.

"Matt! Are you OK?" Marti cried.

"Come here, little girly," the man said as he transferred his attention towards Matt's date.

"Get in the car, quick!" Matt told her, and she dashed to the other side of the car, complied, and locked the door.

Matt made it into the car too. He started the engine, pulled out of the parking lot, and turned onto the street. He hadn't gone a block until he found the man was right behind him in an old Chevy Nova.

Matt could see his adversary's crazed eyes when he looked in the rear-view mirror. He was going as fast as he thought was safe, but the man was right behind them. He was so close he gave the Mustang a shot in the rear that left Matt scrambling for control.

"He's crazy!" Marti cried, turning to watch the Nova out the rear window. "He's trying to wreck us!"

"I know," Matt said. He didn't think he could make it to the police station unscathed, so he headed back to where he knew many police officers were — the bonfire — with his adversary in hot pursuit.

He didn't want to get any of the kids involved, so he headed towards the rear of the park. Nothing was in that particular area except a large pile of firewood on standby.

Seconds before both cars would have crashed into the pile of wood, Matt yanked his steering wheel hard to the left, and his Mustang went nose-first into a small white fence cordoning off the kids' playground.

The man in the Nova never lifted. His car skidded on some wet leaves and plowed hood-first into the pile of wood, sending a host of small logs flying through the air.

Every police officer and volunteer firefighter in the town responded. Matt and Marti told them what happened, and the man was cuffed and hauled off to the holding cell at the police station. The bonfire was extinguished by one of the fire trucks on hand, and everyone went home.

And that's how the case against Stan Anderson for the first-degree murder of Sam Stine broke.

Detective Myers got a search warrant the following day, and found a receipt for aviation fuel in a cardboard box on the floor of Anderson's apartment. He also learned Anderson had a scooter he used for running errands. Black leather chaps and smooth, light-tan leather gloves were found in a white leather bag attached to the back of the scooter. That wasn't unusual, but it explained how Anderson drove to and from the farm over the fields, without being seen on the road. The soft leather gloves left no fingerprints, and they were flame retardant.

As it turned out, they didn't have to work hard to build a case against Anderson. He changed his story three times in the space of an afternoon, but when Detective Myers got tough and confronted him with the facts, he cracked like an egg and confessed to everything. There was an investigation to see what if anything his buddy knew, but it appeared he was clueless, and no charges were filed against him.

The Stines later learned Anderson had been jealous of Matt's grandfather for many years. The trouble began over some farmland Anderson wanted, but Sam had won in an auction right after both had gotten out of the Army. Anderson also admitted to an attraction to fire all his life, but nearly a year later a jury of his peers made sure he'd continue to spend the rest of it behind bars.

4

The Mystery
Of the Silver Wallet

Seventeen-year-old Jeb Mitchell knocked on the door of Sadie Tate's farmhouse deep in Appalachia, and ordered himself to stay calm. He wasn't sure how he'd be received. He'd been on the road early that crisp Saturday morning in October, but she didn't know he was coming.

He could see the crown of Sadie's head covered with mousy gray hair as she peered at him from behind white-lace curtains flanking a dirty window. Jeb doubted Sadie would remember him from the summer, when he'd been part of a youth group from a Louisville, Kentucky church doing a week-long service project in the area. They'd done odd jobs and some construction projects to lend a hand to Sadie and others like her who were struggling to make ends meet.

"Mrs. Tate, it's Jeb, from the church youth group this summer," he said politely and slowly through the door. He wore jeans and a T-shirt under a Cincinnati Bengals hoodie. His blond hair was freshly cut. His blue eyes looked pensive but calm.

His politeness did the trick. Sadie turned the lock, pulled the door open, and peered at him through thick glasses.

"Mrs. Tate, I did some plumbing work in your basement bathroom," Jeb said for further validation. "May I please come in?"

"OK," she said without hesitation.

Three grandchildren who lived with their unwed mother in Sadie's farmhouse were where they'd been the only other time Jeb had been in the room — on the floor in front of an enormous color TV.

"Turn that off!" Sadie ordered.

One girl, about 7, used a remote to turn the TV down but not off.

"What brings you all the way out here?" Sadie asked Jeb. She removed some newspapers from an old green armchair and pointed to it as an invitation for Jeb to sit.

"I heard you lost some money while we were here in July, and I thought I'd see if I could help find it," Jeb said evenly.

There was more to the story. Jeb couldn't believe it when one of the youth group's leaders, Philip Barker, had asked him last Saturday if he knew anything about how Sadie's small metal wallet containing the bulk of her fall property tax payment had gone missing.

Jeb realized he was the only kid who had been on the trip whose family weren't church members, and he was the newest member of the group, but the veiled insinuation still smarted.

Even worse, his next-door neighbor and the reason he'd joined the church group in the first place, Caroline Brady, hadn't stood up for him. She'd been beside him when Mr. Barker had spoken to him, but she'd said nothing in support.

Jeb knew he had faults, but he wasn't a thief. He'd been on a personal campaign of self-improvement for some time now too. He didn't like anyone suspecting him of any wrong doing, let alone stealing from poor people. So he'd asked his father if he could make a quick trip to Appalachia that weekend, thrown a duffel bag containing a couple changes of clothes and some toiletries into the trunk of his Ford Focus, and headed out that morning at 7 a.m.

It was only 127 miles one way, but Booneville, Kentucky was a different world than the suburban Louisville subdivision he called home.

"It was the strangest thing," Sadie said. She looked old, tiny and frail in the cushions of her lumpy sofa. "I had most of the money in a little silver metal wallet. It was about the size of a credit card, only thicker. I remember counting the money to see how much more I had to save before I could pay the second half of the tax bill. But I don't remember putting it back in the top drawer of my bureau, which is where I keep it, and the next time I looked for it, it was gone. The money is due in November," she added sadly.

"May I look at the drawer, ma'am?" Jeb asked.

Sadie led him into her bedroom and pointed to an antique chest of drawers across from an old metal bed. The bed was unmade, and a colorful rag quilt lay in a heap in the middle of it. Like elsewhere throughout the property, there was clutter everywhere.

Jeb didn't know the best way to approach the search. Perhaps the small metal wallet had slipped out of the drawer and was hidden next to its runners. Maybe it was under something else in the drawer.

Jeb emptied the contents of the drawer onto the bed, and together he and Sadie examined everything before putting it all back. Jeb had brought along a flashlight, and he shined it in the space for the drawer before he reinserted it into the bureau. He uncovered nothing but an expired foil of denture-cleaner tablets and some dust.

He moved the heavy bureau too, and shined his flashlight on

the area between the wall and where it had stood, including the previously hidden rug.

Nothing.

"Think back, Mrs. Tate," Jeb said gently. "When was the last time you saw the wallet?"

"I think it was in July when your group was here fixing the bathroom downstairs, and building the deck," she replied. "That's why I contacted the church people. I was hoping someone picked it up by mistake or something."

"OK," Jeb said, ignoring the implications of the 'or something.' "Can you remember anything else that might help us find it?"

"Like what?" Sadie said blankly.

"I don't know," Jeb admitted. "What else were you doing that day? Do you remember what you were wearing?"

"I can't even remember what I was wearing yesterday," Sadie admitted.

"Let's think hard."

They were both aware of the seconds as they passed, marked by an old, charcoal gray, hand-wound Big Ben Timex alarm clock sitting on top of some magazines on top of the bureau.

"You came out to the barn with me once that day to feed your hog, and I think you were wearing an apron with big flowers on it," Jeb suggested.

"I may have; I wear that apron a lot," Sadie agreed.

"Can you show it to me?"

"Yes. It's in the kitchen, hanging on a nail behind the cellar door."

Together they made their way from the bedroom back to the cluttered kitchen. Sadie opened the cellar door, took a light blue apron covered in large, pink cabbage flowers off the nail, and thrust it into Jeb's hands.

"Yes, this is the one," Jeb said.

The apron had ruffles around its shoulder straps that extended the length of its bib, two long ties at the back, and two side pockets.

Jeb slipped a hand into each pocket, hoping to find the wallet.

Nothing.

As his fingers traced the inside of the right pocket, he felt a large spot encircled with thread. He pulled the pocket up closer to his eyes, turned it inside out, and discovered a spot that had been mended.

"Was there a hole in this pocket that you mended, Mrs. Tate?" he asked.

"Yes," Sadie confirmed.

"How long ago was that?" Jeb probed.

"I think it was in August sometime," Sadie related.

"OK," was all Jeb said in reply, but his mind was turning. If the wallet had been in the apron pocket and had fallen out of the hole, it could be anywhere. Sadie was elderly, but she was still active.

Jeb knew this trip had been a long shot. Finding the wallet in the cluttered mess that permeated every room of the farmhouse and the barn was like looking for the proverbial needle in a haystack.

"Since I'm this close, may I use your bathroom in the basement?" Jeb asked. It bought him some time to think, and he wanted to see how his plumbing work was holding up anyway.

"Sure," Sadie agreed.

When he rejoined Sadie in the kitchen, Jeb still wasn't sure where to look next. He moved some empty paper bags and newspapers off a mismatched chair, sat, and faced his host.

"How hard have you looked inside the house?"

"Pretty hard." Sadie took off her glasses and wiped them clean with the hem of her blouse.

"OK. What about outside?"

"Not much. I think it's inside here somewhere. Unless it was stolen."

"OK," Jeb said, ignoring the implication.

The rest of that morning and into the afternoon, Jeb and Sadie scoured the house for the wallet. They broke for lunch, when Sadie prepared hot dogs, potato salad, chips and lemonade for herself, Jeb, the three grandchildren and her daughter, Penny. Jeb found the search hard due to the clutter everywhere, but he kept at it religiously. Unfortunately, they had no luck.

It was after 4 when Jeb decided to head to the barn. He wasn't sure if he would ask Sadie if he could sleep in there tonight or not. He didn't know if it was worth it to keep searching tomorrow. It all seemed like such a lost cause. He'd have to make his mind up soon though, because it was already almost dusk.

A few cold drops of rain spat at Jeb like an angry cat as he opened the barn door and slipped inside. He followed the path he knew Sadie took to the hog pen outside, keeping his eyes peeled for signs of anything shiny that could be the metal wallet.

He opened the rear barn door and looked around. Since it was threatening to rain harder, Lucy, the sow, wasn't flat on her side in her pen soaking up the sunshine. She was upright and looking at him instead, surprised she had a visitor. An abandoned car, its windshield shattered, rusted in silence beyond her pen. The wind was picking up, making the branches of the large oak trees on the opposite side of the pigpen move and moan and their orange leaves rustle. Jeb tried not to notice it was a little spooky.

The ground in the pigpen was as muddy as he recalled. He'd spotted an old shovel hanging next to the barn door, and on a whim, he returned to it and removed it from the wall.

Jeb walked back to the pigpen and felt his sneakers sink a bit in the muck. He hopped the short fence, walked around the trough, and watched Lucy watching him. She grunted, but didn't move any closer.

Jeb stuck the shovel in the mud near the trough and turned a few shovelfuls over. He didn't know why he was looking here, but at least he was doing something. He dug several inches all along the trough without finding anything.

He climbed out of the pen and repeated the process on the other side of the fence. The ground was a little more firm here, and a little less smelly. As he finished each section, he tapped the dirt with the shovel when he was finished, hoping he wasn't contributing to more mud.

He found nothing except some stray glass, a couple of roofing nails, and a shingle.

Disappointed, discouraged, and a little damp from the occasional spits of rain, Jeb took a break and leaned on the top of the shovel's handle. He watched Lucy walk to the trough, anticipating her dinner and wondering if he was going to be the one to deliver it.

"Sorry; I don't have anything for you right now," Jeb told her. He'd heard somewhere that pigs are extremely smart. Lucy seemed to almost understand.

Jeb was cold. As night fell on the barnyard, he knew it was time to give up the search for now. He gave a deep sigh as he looked out over the area. The whole trip had been a long shot, but he had wanted to try.

Out of the corner of his eye, he noticed Lucy rooting through the ground to the right of her trough with her powerful nose. Jeb knew Sadie brought her table scraps daily. She said Lucy loved potato and apple peelings the most. Lucy was probably searching for something tasty that had been left behind yesterday.

As he watched, his eyes grew big when Lucy butted her nose against something, raised her head, and looked straight at him.

Jeb didn't take time to think. He tumbled back over the fence and was beside the large sow in seconds. Reaching through the ooze, his fingers wrapped around the shiny object, and he pulled out the missing wallet.

He knew the money for the fall property taxes would be in it.

He knew he'd just been an enormous help to a family in need.

He knew he'd gone the extra mile and done the right thing.

When the word got out, he knew his status would rise considerably with the members of his youth group, Mr. Barker, and a one Caroline Brady.

And he knew there was something to that notion about the high intelligence of pigs.

5

She's Not Dead Yet

Minerva Stewart put her dinner dishes away, dreading tomorrow. In less than 12 hours she'd be at the bank downtown signing the paperwork that would sell the family farm to a developer. He planned to demolish her house and barn as quickly as possible and replace it with a trucking distribution center.

It was all so upsetting.

Now 80 years old, Minerva had moved into a condo downtown in late April, and suffered through a public auction at the farm in July. The farm had sold quickly when it finally went on the market last month. It was now mid-October. She'd been in her shiny new condo for almost six months.

Through the difficult chore of downsizing and moving, many people assured Minerva she was just starting a new chapter in her life, but it felt more like she was preparing to die. Minerva didn't like that feeling. Although she knew it was inevitable, she didn't want to think about dying.

As she often did in times of discontent, Minerva turned to the Bible for guidance and comfort. Usually she reached for her condensed, easy-to-read version, but tonight she reached for the big family Bible, a King James edition. She'd given it a place of honor in a bookcase in her new living room, to the left of her gas fireplace flickering under a huge, modern, flat-screen TV. A cinnamon candle burned on the mantle, sending out its spicy scent.

Blue veins and age marks stood out on Minerva's papery-thin hands as she turned to the book of Job and read a few chapters. When she turned the next page, she was surprised to discover a thin envelope with her name on it. She opened it slowly, and immediately recognized the handwriting of her late husband, Ralph, on the single page of loose-leaf notebook paper inside.

"Dear Minerva," she read aloud.

"I guess when you find this I'll be dead. I hope you're doing OK. I probably should have told you about this before, but I wanted to find a way to make you happy even after I was gone. Making you happy was a great way to spend my life."

Minerva's eyes misted over, but she blinked and continued to read.

"As you know, I always liked to learn about Abraham Lincoln. There was a personal reason for that other than he was the greatest president we ever had. One of my ancestors was a lady from Maryland who was one of the girlfriends of the actor John Wilkes Booth. When he murdered President Lincoln, he went from being one of the most popular men in America to one of the most hated. My relative was bullied about him, and it became a big family scandal. Finally she couldn't take it anymore, and she committed suicide. She was only in her late twenties when she died.

"I found her diary up in the attic in an old trunk. It's a good story, Minerva, and it tells a lot about that time in American history. I think you should find an author to work on it and publish her story. I think it's so good it could even be a movie.

"I have something else for you too. You always saved your spare change in the piggy bank you kept in the living room. Well, I kept my spare change too, only I put mine in a savings account in the bank. By 1980, I had saved over $10,000. Some of the guys over at the barbershop said I ought to take it out of the bank and invest it in the stock market. I didn't know anything about stocks, but I picked one out because it reminded me of you and your baking, and it did great. The way I figure it, you're very rich now."

Minerva's eyes grew wide, but she kept reading aloud. The only sound was the muffled TV of the young couple that lived next door.

"I didn't want anyone to know about this while I was alive, because I didn't want any big changes to our lives or anyone to steal our stuff, so I hid the diary and the stock papers at the farm," Minerva read on. "Think about your lucky penny and something else we have that's a lot like it, concentrate on the way they're the same, and it will lead you right to it.

"Love, Ralph."

Minerva read the letter again, silently this time. Then she read it silently once more. With each reading her anxiety grew. When she finally set the paper down, she panicked.

How am I going to solve this mystery in one night? she thought. *The farm won't belong to me after tomorrow morning. It's already 10 p.m., pitch black outside, and it's raining to boot.*

Minerva tried to concentrate. *What do I have that is a lot like my lucky penny?* she asked herself. It should never have made it into circulation, because Lincoln's head was cut off on it, right at his neckline.

Minerva paced as she thought, and suddenly she had an idea. *Ralph said that old plaster bust of Lincoln was valuable. I can't imagine how that could be, but the answer has to be with that old piece of junk he cherished* she thought.

The bust was sitting on a shelf on a bookcase flanking the other side of the fireplace. It was the color of brass, although that was only from its glossy gold paint. Minerva carefully took it down, wiped a little dust from it off her hands, and placed it on her new kitchen island where she could get a better look.

Honest Abe stared at her, but divulged nothing.

Minerva picked up the letter again. "Concentrate on the way it's the same as the penny?" Minerva muttered. "What was he talking about?"

Was there some sort of code in the letters on the penny? The bust didn't have any letters, so that couldn't be it.

Lincoln was headless on the penny, but he was intact on the bust.

Minerva picked up the bust and shook it in her frustration. "What are you not telling me?" she cried.

She felt a tiny latch on the base at the back of the statue. She hadn't noticed it before, even when she dusted. It was painted gold, like the bust. She flipped the latch, and the top of the sculpture fell to the side, exposing a red button at the center of the base.

Ralph's clue became clear. The similarity between the sculpture and the penny was that in both cases, now Mr. Lincoln was headless.

What happens when I push this button? Minerva thought as she pushed it.

Nothing happened.

I bet something happens over at the farm though. He said the diary and the stocks are hidden at the farm.

It was now 11 p.m., and Minerva had no time to spare. She turned off the gas logs in her fireplace and blew out her candle. She put the bust in a big orange nylon shopping bag she used at the grocery store. She got her red raincoat and a tan rain hat from the hall closet, and put them on. She grabbed her pocketbook, locked the condo's front door, and headed to her car in the garage.

It wasn't a long trip to the farm, but the conditions were treacherous. Lightning lit the sky and thunder pealed as she drove through torrents of rain towards her destination. The wind blew wickedly through the trees, making their branches and the traffic lights swing. The river was to her right, black as the night, as Minerva drove on like a woman possessed.

Finally she was in front of the farmhouse she'd called home for many years. The steps of the front porch were slippery from the rain, so she was careful and used the handrail as she made her way to the large, wooden front door.

She put her key into the lock, turned it and the knob, and entered the massive living room, now empty. She reached for the light switch, and then remembered she'd had the electricity turned off last week.

That meant another trip to the car for a flashlight, so Minerva retraced her steps and approached the house again. It was still raining hard, and the house looked spooky in the weak beam of the flashlight.

Calm down, Minerva told herself when she was back in the living room.

She put the flashlight into her mouth so she could have both hands free. She reached into her shopping bag, took out the bust, and put it square on the floor. Transferring the flashlight to her left hand, she directed the light onto the red button and pressed it.

With a tiny pop, a section of crown molding near the ceiling opened, and a secret drawer slid out. Without the small noise, she wouldn't have noticed it.

How am I going to get up there? Minerva wondered as she looked at the open drawer near the 14-foot-high ceiling. Ralph must have installed it the last time they painted.

Since the room was devoid of furniture, there was nothing to crawl up on. Resigned, Minerva put her coat and hat back on, and with her flashlight firmly in her hand, she headed for the barn in search of the ladder she'd used last Christmas when she was doing some holiday decorating.

Luckily it hadn't been sold at the auction, and it was where she left it. Minerva slipped once in some mud as she half-carried and half-tugged it into the house, but she didn't fall.

She paused a little to catch her breath before she set the ladder into position, put the flashlight back into her mouth, and started her climb.

The ladder did the trick, but when she was almost to the ceiling, she felt a cold breeze slide by her neck. She wasn't high enough to see what was in the open drawer, but she reached inside with her left hand while holding onto the ladder with her right.

She almost fell off the ladder when another hand gripped her left wrist.

Minerva instinctively shook off the other hand. *How can that be? I must be imagining things!*

She pulled a tan mailing envelope out of the drawer. It was a little brittle, but still serviceable.

She descended the ladder, eased onto the floor, opened the envelope, and dumped a small yellow journal with wispy handwriting and a once-white, business-size envelope onto the hardwood floor.

She already knew whose diary she had, but she was curious about the stocks. Ralph had written something about how he chose them because they reminded him of her baking.

Minerva's eyes grew wide once again when she saw the words "Apple" on the stocks. Ralph had bought stock in Apple Computer because of her award-winning apple pies! She had no idea what a $10,000 investment in 1980 would be worth today, but she knew it had to be a great deal of money.

Minerva put it all back into the envelope, and then put all the papers and the bust into her shopping bag. She climbed up the ladder again and pushed the now-empty drawer shut. On the way down, however, she felt another cold breeze on the back of her neck. When she reached the floor and turned, a pale white woman wearing a white gown with a hooped skirt and a bustle was standing in front of her, looking put out.

Minerva didn't believe in them, but it appeared she was meeting her first ghost.

"Mine," the young woman said, pointing a bony finger at the shopping bag.

Somewhere Minerva had read one had to be firm when dealing with ghosts.

"No, you're dead. It's mine now. I'm not dead yet," Minerva told her firmly, and added politely, "I'll do right by your story."

"See that you do," the ghost said before disappearing in a wisp of vapor.

Minerva shook her gray curls, picked up her shopping bag, put her coat and hat on, locked up, and headed to her car. It was almost 2 a.m. before she was back in her condo, but she was too excited to sleep.

Her whole attitude had changed. In about four hours she'd gone from the despair of Biblical Job to become a multimillionaire, and she'd seen her first ghost.

It was certainly different from last night when I played rummy over at the community center, Minerva marveled to herself. She also thanked her lucky stars she'd thought to buy back her own Lincoln figurine when it went up for sale at her auction at the farm in July.

The money she'd get from the sale of the farm later today would only add to her newfound wealth. Now she was looking forward to the closing, because with a possible book and a movie to produce, and the money to help do it, her farm chores already felt like a distant memory. She could even hire a secretary to keep her on track when her mind wandered.

A whole new chapter of Minerva's life was in front of her. Like she had informed the ghost of a girlfriend of John Wilkes Booth, she wasn't dead yet!

6

One for the Road

"Call the cops. I'll get home as fast as I can. And call me back after you talk to the cops."

Jim Hess lowered his cell phone back onto its black plastic cradle on the dash of the cab of his tractor-trailer truck, frowned, and tried not to panic as he continued to roll west along Interstate 80 in Pennsylvania. He glanced at his terrier, Twister, perched on the seat beside him. They were headed home to Ohio after dropping a load of pumpkins at a distribution center in New York that crisp Saturday afternoon in early October. Jim had been enjoying the fall foliage as the miles clicked by, but now the scenery was the furthest thing from his mind.

The call had been from his wife, Chris. A few minutes ago she'd received an alarming call from the manager of the condo his daughter, Cassie, rented a few miles from their house. The manager said he'd just seen his daughter's ex-fiancé, Rob Jones, drag Cassie from her condo, shove her onto the front seat of his car, and speed away.

Jim had never liked Rob, but he hadn't thought he was a criminal. About 20 minutes later his wife called him back.

"Cassie is too old for an amber alert and too young for a silver alert, but they'll put it out through all their regular channels," Chris told him. "Oh, Jim, I'm so worried."

"I don't think he'll hurt her; he probably just wants to scare her," Jim told her, although he wasn't sure he believed that himself. There was no telling what Rob was capable of. "We have to be calm," he said, swiping his right hand through the right side of his brown hair.

"The cops are going to call you too," Chris told him. "I described her as best I could, but I didn't know what she was wearing. I said she had medium-length brown hair and brown eyes, and was about 5 feet 7."

"I'm sure you did fine. I'll be glad to talk to them; I'm just sitting here twiddling my thumbs on I-80," Jim told her, trying to be as upbeat as possible.

His only daughter lived alone in the same small Ohio town where she'd been raised and where she now worked as a nurse for a family doctor. She'd left Rob at the altar in June. They were both already seeing other people, so this was unexpected.

About an hour later Jim got a call from a Detective Norris.

"Well, at least we know who we're looking for; that's half the battle," the detective said as he rolled some nicotine gum around his mouth. He was tall, with dark hair streaked with gray. "I'm surprised nobody has spotted his car yet."

The detective had a host of questions for Jim, which he answered as well as he could.

As it turned out, it was Jim himself who spotted Rob's old Chevy Malibu about an hour later in the parking lot of a fast-food restaurant in a small town off the interstate. He had a hunch Rob might be headed for his family's hunting cabin in upstate New York. Although Jim didn't know where the cabin was located, many people heading east made a quick stop for food and a restroom break at one particular exit of that highway, and that's where Jim struck pay dirt. He had been climbing back into his cab after a quick break for both he and Twister when Rob's car pulled into the parking lot. Rob had hurried out of the car and into the restaurant.

Jim knew it would be best if he weren't seen, so he inched a little closer to the car with his truck while Rob was inside. His heart dropped when there was no sign of Cassie.

Jim drove across the street to another fast-food restaurant, turned at the back of its parking lot, and positioned his truck so he could still see the Malibu clearly. As soon as he could he reached for the notepad where he'd scribbled Detective Norris's telephone number, and then his cell phone.

"Norris," the detective barked on the second ring.

When he learned it was Jim on the phone, the detective told him they were close to locating Rob through their phone-tracking system.

"I can do better than that," Jim said, and told him where he was and what he'd seen.

"But there's no sign of Cassie," he told the detective sadly.

"Hang in there," Detective Norris told him. "Can you follow him without being seen?"

"Sure."

Jim had been headed west, but Rob entered the eastbound entrance ramp of the interstate a few minutes later, as Jim had predicted. Jim fell in behind him, about six car lengths back.

It's good the little twerp wasn't interested enough in me to even know what trucking company I drive for Jim thought.

Detective Norris was still on the line and wanted any additional information Jim could give him.

"OK; continue to stay behind him," the detective told him. "Keep him in sight, but don't let him see you. I have an idea. I'll get back to you in a few minutes."

The minutes dragged on like a line at Walmart when only one cashier is open. Jim didn't like the fact Cassie wasn't in the car. He wondered if Rob had already murdered her and dumped her body somewhere.

I should have tackled him when I saw him, he thought, although deep down he knew that wouldn't have been best.

Finally Detective Norris called him back and told him his plan.

"Rob doesn't have a CB, does he?" the detective asked.

"No; he never has," Jim told him.

"Can you get on your CB and get two other truckers headed east to help us?" Detective Norris asked.

"10-4," Jim said after Detective Norris told him his plan.

A burly man driving a Con-way Freight truck and a slim trucker for PTL agreed to help right away.

"Hell, this will be fun!" the Con-way trucker said.

"The timing is crucial," Jim told them. "Wait until I get back to you before you move. I have to wait for a signal from the cops."

Back in Ohio, Detective Norris was working quickly. He had to get the Pennsylvania State Police involved, and he didn't have time for any memos.

So that's how two Pennsylvania State Troopers who had been stationed near overpasses looking for speeders were pressed into service.

It was already nightfall, and a full moon was rising. Detective

Norris had Jim recite each mile marker over the phone as he passed them.

It was mere minutes, but it seemed like an eternity to Jim. Finally Detective Norris told him it was time, and Jim passed the message on to the two truckers behind him via their CBs.

The three trucks maneuvered into position around the Malibu, which was in the right-hand lane. The Con-way Freight truck passed the car and slipped into the right lane, directly in front of it. The PTL truck got into the passing lane and hemmed the car in on its left. Jim moved in on the car's rear bumper, and the three trucks surrounded it as they headed into a construction zone.

Following Detective Norris's instructions to perfection, all three truckers rolled to a stop as they approached the road crew's bright, portable lights.

Trapped even though he didn't realize it yet, Rob was forced to do the same. He never saw the two Pennsylvania State Troopers who leaped over the Jersey barriers behind his car, their revolvers drawn, until it was too late. They ran a few paces to the front of the car, aiming their guns through the Malibu's windshield and squarely at Rob's head.

Rob put his car in park and put his hands up. One of the cops opened the car door, dragged him out, and handcuffed him as the other officer continued to point a gun to Rob's head. They marched him to a waiting police cruiser and shoved him into the back of it as Jim climbed down onto the asphalt after ordering Twister to stay.

A couple of impatient motorists who had no idea why the traffic had stopped were already honking when Jim caught some movement at the back of the Malibu out of the corner of his eye.

A small crowbar shattered the car's left taillight from within, and made short circles in the air.

"Cassie!" Jim cried. "Hey! I need help here!"

One of the cops popped the locked trunk lid open less than two minutes later. Cassie, her feet bound with a rope like the one she'd worked loose from her hands, blinked in the bright lights of the construction area. She reached up and unpeeled a length of silver duct tape from her mouth.

"Dad!" she said as he was untying her feet. "How did you get here?"

"Are you OK?" he demanded as he helped her sit up and lifted her out of the trunk. He gave her a quick hug, and kissed the top of her head, not wanting to think about what he could have found inside the trunk.

"I'm OK; just a little rumpled," she replied, her words running together in her excitement. "I've been working on getting that rope off my hands for a long time. His car is so old, there isn't an interior trunk-release latch. How did you find us?"

"Let's get out of this traffic, and I'll fill you in," Jim told her.

"Hey, guys! We can't thank you enough!" he told the two other truckers who were now out of their trucks and standing a little to the side, watching intently. "Let's drive on and pull off at the next rest area, so we're not holding up traffic."

"Nah, that's OK," the Con-way Freight trucker said, and the PTL trucker nodded in agreement. "We gotta keep rolling. Glad everything worked out."

The three men shook hands and headed back to their respective trucks, with Cassie close to Jim.

Detective Norris was still waiting on the other end of Jim's cell phone when they plopped down on the cab's seats. Twister immediately hopped onto Cassie's lap and licked her face.

"It worked out perfectly; it was almost like we had practiced!" Jim told him. "And Cassie was in the trunk; she's fine!"

"Glad this one had a happy ending," Detective Norris said. He clamped down on his gum and smiled. "You can always count on there being construction zones on the interstates in Pennsylvania."

7

Where There's a Will, There's a Way

Doreen looked up from Cheryl's old laptop, stretched, and rotated her head. She'd been working on her math homework for her online high-school equivalency degree for an hour, but a few minutes ago she'd stopped to search the Internet for anything new in a homicide case that had been on yesterday's local news.

The case intrigued her. She knew the odds of a homeless woman like herself locating a murderer were slim, but she wanted to try.

Who am I kidding? Even if I found him, I couldn't chase him, she thought. *I don't even have a car. Whoever heard of someone doing a police chase while walking or taking the bus?*

She smiled at the idea, but it didn't deter her.

Cheryl, a volunteer at the homeless shelter where Doreen had been staying with her young son for almost a year, had been infectious with her constant, positive coaching. She repeatedly advised Doreen to build upon her strengths instead of focusing on what she didn't have.

What I have going for me is I know a lot of people on the streets who might have seen something, Doreen thought. *That's where I need to start. And if I solve this mystery, it could help me get a job with the police department.*

The victim was a young woman a little older than Doreen who lived in an apartment building two blocks from the shelter. Doreen had never met Stacey Wilson, but she knew the yellow brick building well. Doreen and her son, Davey, had slept in its courtyard occasionally when they were on the streets. Life was far better at the shelter, and Doreen had been making great progress in getting clean from her addictions and building a life for herself and her son with the help she was receiving there.

The next afternoon she had time to make some inquiries. Bundling up in jeans and a red sweater she had bought at Goodwill over the summer, she used the bright autumn afternoon to take a stroll around the neighborhood. She was glad she'd exchanged her usual high heels for sneakers. Her long fingernails were painted in alternating colors of neon orange and black for Halloween. Her hair was usually dyed pink, but today it was a shimmering neon blue like a summertime Popsicle.

Larry Martin, a city cop who had arrested Doreen for vagrancy once, was right where she thought he'd be around 2 p.m. — in the line for doughnuts at Hoover's Bakery. Larry had been respectful when he'd arrested Doreen a little more than a year ago. She now considered him a casual friend. On the wall beside him was a cardboard cutout of a black cat wearing a black witch's hat. A tissue-paper honeycomb ghost dangled on a string above him, swinging in the breeze from a ceiling vent nearby. The scent of cinnamon sugar permeated the air.

Larry let a couple of people go ahead of him so Doreen was right behind him in line as they stood beside large wooden cases laden with pastries. After some light banter, Doreen got to her point very innocently. "What do you know about the Wilson case?" she asked.

"Not much. Homicide has it," Larry replied, reaching into his wallet to see how many ones he had. "As far as I know they don't have any leads, or the murder weapon."

"She was shot, right?" Doreen asked.

"Yeah; I heard forensics said it was a Glock 30," Larry said.

"Any ideas on a motive?" Doreen pressed on.

"Not really, that I heard," Larry said. "Hey, why the big interest?"

"Oh, nothing; just exploring police work as a possible career choice." Doreen said it so flippantly Larry didn't realize she was telling the truth.

The pair placed their doughnut orders. Larry treated Doreen to a pumpkin spice latte topped with cinnamon too, and they parted with their respective waxy white bags.

Doreen sipped the latte as she strolled to a park about five blocks away. It was an extravagant treat. She savored each swallow of the creamy, rich, slightly spicy beverage.

Doreen knew most of the homeless people in the area would be at the park now, waiting for the free bread to be delivered by the church group that supplied leftovers from area bakeries every other day. It didn't take her long to arrive, or to find Tony Devine, a homeless man who usually knew the latest gossip.

After some small talk, Tony disclosed the police had interviewed Highway Jim about his whereabouts the night of the murder.

"They didn't bring him in, but they quizzed him," Tony told her. "His priors made him a suspect, but none of us think he did it."

"What do you know about the woman that got shot?" Doreen asked.

"Not much," Tony said. "I think she was gay. She lived alone, but that girl who works at your shelter knew her. Highway Jim said he saw her going into her apartment several times."

"Somebody who works at the shelter? Who?" Doreen asked, peeling a little nail polish off one of her long fingernails.

"I don't know; ask Highway Jim," Tony said.

"Where is he?" Doreen pressed.

"I think he's panhandling over by the interstate, but he should be at the overpass tonight," Tony advised.

Highway Jim was one of many of the area's homeless who resisted going into a shelter unless the weather was particularly bad. They preferred to stay independent, and in the evenings they could usually be found under an overpass of the highway about a mile further east.

"OK; thanks for the info," Doreen told Tony, preparing to leave.

The church group hadn't arrived yet, so Tony wasn't busy. "How is your little boy?"

"We're both doing really well; thanks for asking!"

"You look good," Tony replied, without caring how Doreen took it.

"Thanks!" Doreen said automatically, but she appreciated the compliment.

Doreen knew Highway Jim was a night owl, so she didn't leave the shelter until a little after midnight. She was wearing a fleece jacket with a hood, but the wind cut through her as she hurried along.

It was threatening to rain. She had found a black umbrella in a closet at the shelter, and she opened it above her head even though two of its spokes were broken. She lurched down the street with her cockeyed umbrella like an injured spider trying to escape even though it was missing a couple legs.

It wasn't a good night for a hike. The moon peeked out of dark clouds now and then, and those clouds spit out some intermittent rain. There weren't many streetlights, but Doreen had brought along a flashlight. Its beam was weak, and it made eerie shadows wherever she shined it.

She shivered from both the night air and the neighborhood. There were no sidewalks here, so she had to be careful of her footing.

Finally she reached the overpass. Trucks overhead rumbled as they hit potholes without slowing. Their headlights cut through the darkness, making strobe-light passes as they flew by.

She passed a few homeless people who didn't look familiar, nodded, and kept on going.

She found Highway Jim set up against the north wall of the overpass. Tonight was his laundry night. A small red plastic bucket of water was to his right, and boxer shorts and a pair of socks were air-drying on a piece of twine he'd strung between two nails in the concrete wall. He was bundled up in a worn, dark-green parka, and he was wearing a red-plaid trapper hat. Its wide black ties hung next to his cheeks, making him resemble a basset hound with droopy ears.

"Hey, Highway Jim!" Doreen greeted him warmly.

Talking to Highway Jim was always a 50-50 proposition. Sometimes he was so high he just looked at people in a stupor. Other times he talked so fast no one could understand him. The laundry was a good sign he was coherent tonight.

"Hey, is that you, Doreen?" he replied, squinting in the weak beam of her flashlight.

"Sure is!"

"Well, what the hell! How are you?"

"Great!" she replied. "Davey and I are both doing better. How are you?"

"Just another day in paradise," Highway Jim said, blinking his bleary gray eyes.

"I dropped by because I was wondering if you knew anything about the lady that got murdered over at Park Court?"

By the startled look on his face, Doreen realized she'd broached the subject too quickly. She should have warmed him up with a little more small talk.

"Who says I know anything about that?" Highway Jim said warily.

"Oh, nobody," Doreen assured him. "But Tony said that woman was friends with somebody at the shelter, and you might know who."

"I might," Highway Jim agreed, after a short pause. His lips were open a little, and Doreen could see the tip of his tongue.

"Sure is windy," Doreen said, having learned her lesson. "It looks a lot like Halloween."

"It must be October now, right?" Highway Jim wanted to know.

"Yeah; it's the 19th."

"Hmm," Highway Jim nodded.

A couple minutes passed in companionable silence until Highway Jim opened up.

"Well, no need for both of us to get pneumonia," he said. "More than once I saw that Lillian woman go into the apartment of the girl that got killed," he said. "I think they're both gay, and had a thing going."

"Lillian Hall? Gay? I never knew," Doreen said. "She never talks about her personal life. She just wants to know all about ours."

"Well, it's only what I think," Highway Jim replied. "I don't know for sure."

"Interesting," Doreen said. "That's something I'll check out, for sure. Thank you!"

"You're welcome," Highway Jim said. "Now don't be a stranger, you hear?"

"Sure thing, Highway Jim," Doreen said. "You take care of yourself, and I'll see you around."

She was so happy she gave him a little hug before she left. He beamed like a schoolboy who just found out he could have two desserts at dinner.

As Doreen hurried back to the shelter, she reviewed what she knew. She didn't even have circumstantial evidence. All she had were hunches.

Well, I'm still going to check them out, she vowed.

She overslept the next morning a little, but by 10 a.m. she knew Lillian wasn't going to be at the shelter today to perform her job as social worker/therapist.

"She hasn't been in her office for several days," disclosed Charles, the shelter's 80-something receptionist. "I think she's in Chicago. Mr. Burt said something about her mother being sick."

"Hmm," Doreen said. She was going to have to be nonchalant to get into Lillian's locked office.

Although it wasn't her day to clean, later that afternoon Doreen rolled an industrial black plastic bucket on wheels that was filled with sudsy water and a mop over to Charles' station near the front door. A roll of paper towels and an empty plastic trash bag were tucked between her left arm and chest.

"Charles, Mr. Burt asked me to clean some windows," she lied. "Could you let me into Miss Lillian's office? I thought I'd start there while she was out."

Her story seemed plausible to Charles. He slowly took his heavy key ring off his belt, found the right key out of about 30 possibilities, and let Doreen into Lillian's office.

"Be sure to lock up when you're done," he told her.

"Will do," Doreen replied.

Inside, she worked quickly. Most of Lillian's file cabinets were locked, but there were piles of files and magazines scattered throughout the small office. Her desk was unlocked, but its contents were just the usual office supplies.

I don't even know what I'm looking for, Doreen admitted.

She realized she'd be questioned later if the windows weren't clean, so she got to work. There were only two windows in the room. They were both large though, and it took her about a half hour to finish the job.

As she put the last of the used paper towels into the waste can by Lillian's desk, she noticed it was full, so she emptied it into the larger trash bag she'd brought with her. As she was dumping the contents of the can into the bag, a small metal object flashed by among the papers and used towels.

What's that? she asked herself as she picked up a small cartridge.

It's a magazine from a gun! she realized, her eyes growing wide. *That's not your usual office item.*

She stuffed the cartridge into the right-front pocket of her jeans.

I don't have much time left, but let's see what's in that closet, she thought.

She rifled through some boxes of files and receipts, unimpressed. A pink photo box decorated with the word 'Paris' in many different fonts looked interesting. She lifted the lid and found a variety of Lillian's personal photos. She sorted through them until she found a photo of two young women holding hands in front of Cinderella's

Castle at Disney World. 'Lillian and Stacey, June 2015,' was written on the back in Lillian's handwriting.

If that's the victim, it's proof they knew each other, Doreen thought.

She carefully put the photo in the left-front pocket of her jeans and left the room, setting the lock on the door before she pulled it shut.

Her next visit was to the administrator of the shelter, Burt Baxter, who was fondly called Mr. Burt by many of the shelter's staff members and guests.

"Do you know where Lillian is?" she asked him innocently.

"She called off all this week; her mother had a stroke, so she went to be with her in Chicago," Mr. Burt said. "You can also talk to Cheryl or me," he added, since Lillian was Doreen's therapist.

"Oh, it's not that; I was just wondering," Doreen assured him.

When she was back in the study room and alone, Doreen pulled the gun magazine and the photo out of her pockets and laid them beside Cheryl's laptop.

She picked them up, one by one, and examined them.

The photo didn't disclose anything new.

The magazine had a dent on one side, making her think Lillian might have discarded it because it was damaged. She also found 'Glock 21' stamped in black type on the bottom of it.

That isn't right, she thought. *Larry said Stacey had been killed with a Glock 30. And where is the gun?*

Doreen didn't know much about handguns, so she did an Internet search to try to learn more. In less than 20 minutes she discovered the magazine of a Glock 21 would also fit into a Glock 30.

She decided it was time to tell what she knew, so she called the precinct and asked for Larry. Luckily he was in, finishing some paperwork. After a short conversation, he told her to come to the station and together they'd visit the homicide office, so Doreen headed out with the magazine and the photo in her pockets. She arrived a short bus ride later, met Larry, and together they walked into Detective Murray's office.

Detective Murray wasn't much older than Larry. He listened intently to what Doreen had to say.

"You might be on to something; I'll check it out," he said. "Thank you for telling us what you know."

"Well, they always say 'Anyone with any information should contact the police,'" Doreen replied. "Plus, I'd like to work in law enforcement someday."

"I think you're on your way," Larry said, and Detective Murray nodded in agreement.

In less than 24 hours, Detective Murray learned Lillian's mother hadn't had a stroke, and Lillian was not in Chicago. Lillian was the co-signer of Stacey's checking account, which she'd drained. She was also the sole beneficiary of Stacey's will, which would give her Stacey's sizeable trust fund upon her death. Lillian had flown to Cozumel the night before Stacey's body had been discovered, but still had plenty of time to commit the murder.

The following day, Mexican police officers arrested Lillian in her hotel room. A Glock 30 was in her suitcase.

Some time in a Mexican jail did the trick. By the time Lillian was escorted back to the States in handcuffs, accompanied by an armed guard, she had confessed. She admitted she had a gambling problem, and said she and Stacey had argued so much about their money problems that she had turned to murder.

The police department gave Doreen a commendation certificate for her help in breaking the case. The chief of police presented it to her in his office, and a local TV station was on hand to document how the homeless community had helped break the case.

Doreen was quick to tell the chief of police and the TV reporter about her career aspirations. The police chief told her it was a good career choice, and said she should give him a call once she had her high school diploma.

"It might be a secretarial position to start, but we'll see if we can find some scholarships to help you with the police academy," he promised.

"You'll have to trim those fingernails though," he added with a smile. Doreen's long nails were a bright blue that day.

Doreen told Cheryl the whole story in detail the next day when they met in the shelter's rec room. Surprisingly, Cheryl's mother had been along and had been pleasant to them both. Doreen knew Cheryl and her mother hadn't gotten along well in the past, but they both were trying to build a new, more healthy relationship.

"So Lillian murdered her partner to get her trust fund?" Cheryl repeated.

"Yeah. Where there's a will, there's a way, both for her and for me," Doreen said, and all three women smiled.

8

Deep Down on the Farm

For some strange reason, Rick Hunley remembered their technical name from his high school science class. The large seams of limestone jutting out of the earth in the pasture of his small Pennsylvania farm were "residual boulders."

He hadn't paid much attention in that class, and he'd paid even less attention to those gray and white rock formations until last Saturday.

It was early November, but the unseasonably warm weather had given him time to plant two blue spruce trees next to his driveway at the front of his property. When he was finished, one of his dogs, Buster, forced him to check the rocky area out back by barking incessantly. The German Shepherd mixed with God-knows-what had pointed him to a large hole between two boulders. Rick convinced Buster to leave it alone then, but now, a week later, he had the time to return to the spot to investigate.

Buster was pleased. He sniffed at everything within range as Rick approached the hole. His other dog, Percy, another mutt whose mother or father was probably a border collie, went along with the program happily, like always. It was much colder now than it had been last Saturday, and Rick was glad he'd gotten the trees planted when he did.

He was surprised to see how large the hole was. He wasn't surprised it existed because he knew there were caverns in the area, but he wondered why he hadn't noticed a hole this big on his property in the past.

Although Rick was 6 feet tall, it wouldn't take much for him to crawl inside it. He promised himself he wouldn't go far, but his curiosity was spiked. He turned on the powerful flashlight he'd borrowed from his SUV, hiked up his jeans, and got ready to go inside.

"Stay!" he ordered Buster and Percy as he rubbed his short brown beard. The dogs cocked their heads to ask him to reconsider letting them go along, but obeyed.

Rick put the flashlight in his mouth and crawled inside the hole, flat on his stomach. The seams of limestone continued horizontally for about 20 feet. After he had inched along that far and passed a colony of centipedes, the hole got larger, and he was able to proceed on his hands and knees. While he was in that position he came across the biggest spider he'd ever seen and gave it plenty of room. Twenty feet later the corridor grew larger still. Before long he could stand upright, and he transferred the flashlight from his mouth to his right hand.

Although the underground corridor was cool, the exertion Rick had applied to get this far left him out of breath. The air was musty and damp, and the primary odor was of earth and rock. As he swept the hallway-like room with his flashlight, he noticed the limestone walls were damp, and the once dusty dirt at his feet was now a little spongy.

I'll go a little more and then turn around, Rick told himself. He hadn't gone 100 more feet when he entered a large underground room and stopped in his tracks, horrified.

A human skeleton was propped up on the wall directly ahead of him. A snake was coiled up in what was left of its rib cage.

Rick's heart raced. *No sudden movements,* he told himself, trying his best to calm down. *Most snakes aren't poisonous. They usually won't do anything to you if you leave them alone. And they only eat now and then,* he thought.

Apparently this was now, or perhaps it was then. Suddenly the snake darted out of the dead man's bones and stunned a rat Rick hadn't noticed. After a short, violent struggle the snake started to pull the rat into his mouth, inch by inch. Rick stood and watched, spooked and yet mesmerized as the rat, dazed but still alive, slowly disappeared.

Rick gulped once, simultaneously with the snake.

I'm out of here, Rick thought as he backed away, still staring at the snake and the skeleton. By now most of the rat's body was already inside the snake. Only its hairless tail dangled out of the snake's mouth, although it was hard to see because it was the same dusty color as the skeleton's rib bones.

I wonder if that used to be Old Man Lyons? Rick thought. He had purchased the property several years ago from the estate of Larry Lyons, who had disappeared five years earlier after a local scandal. The prevalent theory at the time was Lyons had run away to El Salvador with a local barmaid. Rick had never given any of it much thought after the real estate closing.

Rick was still watching the bump in the snake's body that was what was left of the rat when he realized he could hear water rushing in the distance, straight ahead.

I wonder if that's an underground stream? he thought.

His curiosity got the best of him. He continued further ahead, leaving the room with the dead man, the reptile, and what was left of the rodent.

The ground at Rick's feet was getting wetter. At one point he slipped and got both his boots and his socks wet when he fell into a small stream of water flowing next to the natural path. Small streaks of red clay stuck to his white socks in several layers like the red and orange streaks on the rock walls surrounding him.

Damn! I need to watch where I'm going! he admonished himself. *I don't want to break a bone while I'm down here.*

That thought was still in his head when he suddenly stopped just in time, on the edge of a cliff. He moved his flashlight around. A large underground room spread out beneath him, complete with stalactites and stalagmites. The rock walls were wet, he was now standing in mud, and the water he had heard was a roaring underground river about 70 feet below him.

Wow! Rick thought, in awe of the place. *But that's it! I need to get back right away.*

At that moment a bat took exception to his intrusion and dove down on him angrily. It flew so close Rick could see its beady eyes, the pink and gray membranes of its wings, and even its tiny teeth. Rick instinctively threw his arms up to protect his head from the bat, and his flashlight went flying dizzily. It struck a stalactite and tumbled down the cliff. The plastic cover and bulb broke when it hit the wall as it bounced, and Rick's world went dark.

"Damn!" Rick said aloud, his voice echoing in the cavern.

For several seconds he could both hear and feel his pounding heart. He struggled to remain calm. It was pitch black, and terror was taking hold.

The only way out of this is to feel along, and hope I'm guessing right on the direction, he told himself. *I need to try not to panic.*

He turned around on the tiny bit of limestone he was standing on, felt for the rock wall, and eased his way back towards the room with the dead man. It was tough going in the dark, and complete fear was taking hold. He realized how cold he was, especially since his socks and boots were wet. He was thirsty too. He wished he'd brought a bottle of water with him. The exertion plus the fear that was threatening to overpower him made his throat feel parched, and his mouth was like cotton.

He still had his cell phone, but he knew it wouldn't work. He had poor reception in his own living room because the farm was far from any cellular towers.

His thoughts drifted to Kate Martin, a girl he'd started seeing over the summer. She was away for the weekend, competing in a horse show, and wouldn't even try to check in until Sunday night at the earliest.

Rick shook his head and continued to grope along. His fingers skimmed along the slippery walls of stone in the dark, and he felt the heavy mineral content in the damp air. His feet, so quick to explore the path ahead a few minutes ago, were now heavy due to his fear and the wet and cold. He shivered through his flannel shirt and cotton sweatshirt, which were both filthy from the crawling he'd done earlier.

It's cold! I wasn't smart about any of this, Rick chastised himself. *I need to get out of here, so I don't end up like Old Man Lyons. I wish I would have told somebody what I was doing before I left.*

Although that was true, it wasn't helping. *I have to think straight and retrace my way. Don't panic!*

He inched along, and finally thought he'd reached the room with the skeleton. He couldn't see anything, but it seemed to be about the correct distance, and the path felt much wider.

When he bumped into a boulder, he took the opportunity to sit for a minute on it and catch his breath. He didn't like being close to the skeleton or the snake and unable to see them.

His body and his brain felt numb. He realized he was exhausted, and a prime candidate for hypothermia. He knew it was best to keep going, but he was so tired. Making it to this room had been hard, and he had so far to go.

I'll rest for just a bit, he bargained with himself.

Darkness does things to a person's mind. When coupled with acute fear, the result is even stranger.

Rick didn't know if he was dreaming or hallucinating, but it felt like his two brothers, Craig and Jeff, were in the cave now too. Both had been killed in traffic accidents. He'd lost Jeff less than a year ago, right before Christmas.

Rick didn't believe in ghosts and he didn't see one, but he was convinced his brothers were with him. Time slowed to a crawl as he tried to figure out what was happening. It was crazy, but it was also comforting. And then he lost all concept of time as he fell into a fitful sleep.

Unbeknown to Rick as he slept, hours passed.

Suddenly he awoke; there was water in his mouth. He gulped and opened his eyes, his arms flaying wildly at a bright light ahead of him.

He thought it might be heaven.

As his eyes and his brain focused, he realized the light was the beam from a lantern sitting on the top of a hard hat worn by a complete stranger who was very much alive.

"You OK, man?" the stranger, who was about the same age as

Rick, asked him as he lifted a now-empty plastic bottle of water from Rick's lips.

"I think so," Rick answered, coughing up some of the water.

"Well, let's get you out of here," the stranger said. "My name is Tim Young. I explore caves as a hobby, and I have to tell you that you went about this all wrong."

Tim then chewed Rick out for his foolhardiness.

"If you want to explore a cave, join our club and learn how to do it the right way, so nobody has to save your hide," Tim told him.

Rick smiled weakly and nodded in agreement.

He took the energy bars Tim provided, as well as the dry socks and small blanket that came out of the numerous pockets dotting Tim's coat.

"Any idea who your buddy is?" Tim asked him, nodding to the skeleton. "He's been dead for awhile."

"I think it might be Larry Lyons, who used to own this property," Rick told him.

"Well, we'll tell the cops about him when we get on top," Tim replied. "Can you make it now?"

"Yes, sir!" Rick said. "How did you find me, anyway?"

"You weren't hard to track," Tim told him. "I got the call to go looking for you after your neighbors called the cops. They noticed your dogs were sitting on a bunch of limestone in your pasture all day, and your SUV hadn't moved," Tim explained. "You better reward those dogs when we get out because they stayed put all day."

"Yes, sir!" Rick repeated, and added one thing so Tim would know he wasn't a total idiot.

"They're residual boulders," he said, and both men smiled as they started the trip back to the surface.

9

Once Under a Mattress, At Sea

Maria Ricardo had never set foot on a cruise ship before this morning. She'd never dined at the captain's table until a couple hours ago. She'd never gone to bed in a swanky cabin on Empress Cruise Line's Emerald of the Seas until a few minutes ago. She had many years of experience working as a hotel housekeeper, however, and some stains on the carpeting beside her bed were bothering her so much that she couldn't get to sleep.

She tried to ignore them, and then gave up. She peeled the champagne-colored silk comforter off her tiny body, crawled out from between the matching 1,000-thread-count sheets, and sank to her knees on the cabin's thick carpeting to get a closer look.

The stains were mostly dark dots. There was a bigger smear leading under the bed, however, so she raised the matching bed skirt to get a better look.

As her brown eyes focused in the dim light, they grew wide. She thought she screamed, but no sound came out of her mouth.

The body of a well-dressed woman was lying in a pool of blood under her mattress.

Within seconds Maria recognized the dead person. It was Felicia Graham, whom she'd met not three hours ago at dinner at the captain's table.

Maria was still in her nightgown and bare feet as she pounded on the door of the adjacent cabin, which was occupied by her youngest son, Seb. They'd won the cruise this summer from the Indianapolis Indians minor-league baseball team as a thank you for Seb's past service in the U.S. Army. November may have been an unusual time to take a cruise, but it was the best time for them both to get off work. Seb hadn't even balked at the idea of taking a cruise with his mom, as they had always had a special connection.

"Seb! Help!" Maria cried. Seconds later Seb opened the door, grabbing his pants lying on a chair with his other hand in the process.

"There's a dead woman under my bed!" Maria told him.

Two hours later, after Seb got the purser, who alerted the ship's head of security, who alerted the captain himself, Maria was in another room further down the hall, now wearing one of Seb's T-shirts, his running shorts and flip-flops. The body was now on a tarp on top of the mattress in her former room, and the door was locked.

The security officer had alerted the police in the nearest port, who would transfer the body to their morgue in the morning. Maria's former room was now being treated as a crime scene, and Maria and Seb had both been to a meeting in the captain's office that night. They were asked not to discuss what had happened with the other passengers so the security officer could do his work, and no panic would ensue among the passengers. It was left unspoken, but Maria and Seb both understood the cruise line wanted to avoid adverse publicity if at all possible.

Captain Hines had been more than nice. He asked them both if they wanted to continue the cruise or if they'd like the cruise line to fly them back to their home in Indianapolis, free of charge. He said no matter what, they'd both be receiving a free cruise sometime in the future to make up for the trauma they'd faced tonight.

Maria's clothes were locked in her former room for now, but Paul Norton, the ship's security officer, would transfer her clothing and luggage to her new room within the hour.

Mr. Norton had asked Maria and Seb if they had ever met Ms. Graham before tonight, and if they had any idea who would want to kill her. He also asked them when they'd left the main dining room and where they'd gone afterwards, recording their responses in a small, black notebook.

"I never met her before tonight at dinner, but I noticed her beautiful ring, and complimented her on it," Maria said as she thrust her right hand through her short black hair. "It is in the shape of a starfish. The body of the starfish is done in opals, and there are smaller pearls and diamonds beside it," she continued. "I think the ring is real, not costume jewelry. I don't think the motive of the murder was a burglary though because she was still wearing the ring when she was under my bed."

"What did Ms. Graham say when you commented on her ring?" Mr. Norton asked.

"She just said 'thank you' in a kind of snippy way, so I left her alone after that," Maria said, tilting her head towards the door.

"I never even talked to her," Seb said. "She was sitting on the other side of the table, too far away from me."

Late the following morning Mr. Norton called Maria's new room and asked if he could drop by to ask her some more questions.

"Sure," Maria said. "I have nothing to hide."

During that meeting, Mr. Norton disclosed Ms. Graham had died by a bullet to her heart from a small handgun like a woman would carry. He said he had no leads at the moment, but he was checking out the story of a deckhand who Ms. Graham had reprimanded earlier that day. There had also been two unsolved murders recently at a nearby port, but he doubted anyone could get on board the cruise ship without the proper credentials.

"She doesn't seem to have any family, and we haven't come up with any friends yet either," Mr. Norton said. "We're still trying to find out how she made a living. The only thing everyone agrees on is that she was a complainer."

"You can speak frankly with me," Maria said. "When I met her, I got the impression she was not very nice. However, she still didn't deserve to be murdered."

"No," Mr. Norton agreed. "I need to find the murder weapon," he admitted. "If you can think of anything that might help me with this case, please be sure to speak up, no matter how inconsequential you think it might be," he asked, and Maria assured him she would.

Later that night, after a nice afternoon by the pool and a relaxing massage in the ship's spa followed by a steak dinner and a show at the ship's theater, Maria and Seb stopped for drinks in one of the ship's bars before heading back to their rooms. The bar was decorated like an old Irish or English pub, with dark-paneled walls, mahogany furniture, dark-green furnishings and brass accents.

During a casual conversation with the bartender, they learned that particular bar was going to undergo a renovation the next time the ship was in dock.

"It's a shame; I hope they don't throw out all these old photos," the bartender said. "Some of them date back to the ship's construction, and our maiden cruise."

"How long have you been working on this ship?" Seb asked him.

"Since the first cruise," he answered. "There are only two of us left from those days; me and Captain Hines."

"Really?" Seb asked.

"Yes," the bartender answered. "I have a picture from those old days."

He reached over some liquor bottles on a shelf behind the bar, took down a large photo in an ornate, gold frame, and placed it on the bar in front of them.

"This is this bar on this ship's first cruise," he said. "That's me, behind the bar, and sitting where you're sitting now is Captain Hines."

Seb and Maria looked closer, and Maria caught her breath. Sitting next to the captain was a much younger Felicia Graham. Maria wouldn't have recognized her except she was wearing the same starfish ring she was wearing the night she was murdered.

Seb hadn't made the connection, and Maria tried hard to be cool. After a few minutes passed, she casually asked the bartender if he knew whom the woman was seated next to the captain in the photo.

"Oh, that was his girlfriend at the time," the bartender said. "I don't remember her name. Luckily he never married her; she wasn't very nice."

"Oh," was all Maria said, and the conversation moved on to other changes made to the ship over the years.

True to her word, Maria did what she had promised, and told Mr. Norton about the captain's connection to the deceased the next morning. He thanked her, and again wrote notes in his black notebook.

"Do you have any leads?" Maria asked him.

"I'm checking out a few ideas," was all Mr. Norton would say.

Maria was surprised no one from the nearest port had even come on board to interview her. It made her wonder about the safety of all cruise ship passengers, who like her would remain oblivious unless something like this happened to them.

That afternoon marked the midway point of the short cruise. Being a hard worker all her life, Maria had already grown tired of a life of leisure. Seb was still enamored with the 24-hour buffets offering every food item possible under the hot Caribbean sun, but Maria was already wondering what was going on at home and at work in Indianapolis. She also missed her grandchildren.

Vacationing was so new to her that Maria was more antsy than relaxed. She knew she shouldn't do it, but the lure of the mystery was too much for her, and she decided to take matters into her own hands. Through her work, she'd learned how to pick locks with a credit card. When the coast was clear, she slipped down the hall to her former cabin. In a few seconds, she let herself into her original room.

Now, where would I hide a gun in here? Maria asked herself as she surveyed the room. The body had been transferred to the morgue at their next port without the passengers' knowledge, but Maria found the atmosphere was still eerie. Some bloodstains still dotted the carpet like little reminders of the life that had ended here.

Maria looked in all the cabin's cupboards with no luck. She investigated the bathroom next, with the same results. She was standing in the middle of the small cabin, hands on her hips, considering all the options, when she heard someone in the hall outside turn a key in the lock of the cabin's main door.

I need to hide, fast! Maria thought. *But where?*

Suddenly she was grateful she was 4-feet, 8-inches tall and weighed less than 100 pounds. She slipped behind a table beside a picture window providing a view of the ocean. The table was covered with a white tablecloth, which helped keep her hidden. There was enough room for her to see what was going on with one eye, while the rest of her body was concealed.

She could hardly believe her eyes when Captain Hines slipped into the room. He wore casual clothes, not his uniform. Without hesitation, he stretched his right arm as high as possible and withdrew a tiny silver handgun from the glass base of the room's ceiling light fixture. It had been leaning out of sight on the metal spokes of the fixture. He unloaded the gun's bullets and put them and the gun in the right-side pocket of his pants. Less than a minute later he was gone, locking the door behind him.

Seb, meanwhile, was on a lounge chair, enjoying the view of the bikinis in and beside the ship's main pool.

"What are you reading?" a lanky, red-haired girl in a yellow swimsuit who was about his age asked him.

"It's a book of short stories I bought at a store at the Indianapolis Airport before I flew down here," Seb told her. "It's called 'Twelve Stories for Summer.' Even though it's November, I thought it would help me get in the mood for a tropical cruise."

"Is it any good?" she asked.

"I'd give it five stars, and I'm only a third of the way through it," he said. "It's part of a four-book series. I plan on buying the other three books too. They're quick reads."

His cell phone rang. The caller ID indicated it was his mom on the other end, so he excused himself from the girl and answered the phone on its second ring.

"Captain Hines just left my first room with a gun, and he's headed down the hall towards the theater," Maria reported in one breath. "He's not in his uniform; he's wearing jeans and a blue sports shirt. I'll call Mr. Norton, but you follow him, please! And be careful!" she added quickly.

"Yes, sir! I mean Mom," said Seb, who left everything on a white-metal end table and took off towards the hall.

Seb caught sight of the captain a few minutes later. He was outside on the deck, a lone figure between two lifeboats in a line of eight suspended over the deck and dangling a few feet from the floor. Seb ducked behind the first one to stay hidden and yet still see what the captain was about to do.

At first Seb thought Captain Hines might be climbing into a lifeboat, but he quickly surmised the captain was intent not on a getaway, but on destroying the evidence. He was about to drop the gun into the ocean when Seb tackled him from behind.

The pair struggled against the lifeboats for a few minutes, but the captain was no match for Seb, who had been fighting terrorists in Afghanistan for the U.S. Army less than four months ago.

"Give the gun up, Captain," Seb advised him, and the weapon dropped to the deck. "It's over."

Mr. Norton padded up, with a huffing Maria right behind him. Mr. Norton took the gun, put the captain in handcuffs and read him his rights, and the quartet proceeded to Mr. Norton's office.

That was Captain Hines' last day at sea. As it turned out, Felicia Graham had been blackmailing him for years over some smuggling scheme she'd gotten him involved in years ago in Panama. He hadn't expected her on board his ship, let alone at his table for dinner. When he saw her in a hallway a little later, they argued and he snapped. He took Felicia's own gun out of her designer purse, shot her, and stuffed her body under the bed of the nearest cabin.

Captain Hines did six years in jail and 10 more on probation for her murder. His sentence was drastically reduced due to Felicia blackmailing him, his good behavior in prison, and an expensive attorney. He lost his house to pay his legal bills, but once his past was finally behind him, he rebuilt his life. He did get a pension from the cruise line, and he supplemented that income by selling jet skis for a small company near Miami.

Maria went back to her job in housekeeping at the Hampton Inn near the Indianapolis Airport. She's planning to take her second free cruise sometime next year. She has also started a savings account so her whole family can go on a cruise together sometime in the future.

Seb is training to be an Indiana State Trooper. He's saving his free cruise for his honeymoon after he finds the right girl, who will be someone a lot like his tenacious mom.

10

A Major Mystery

As tractor-trailer trucks whizzed by them on the Staten Island Expressway on a crisp Saturday afternoon in October, three young women on horseback made their way down a sandy path near the landfill at different speeds of a walk. A small, dark-bay Thoroughbred with a blaze on its face led the way, followed by another well-behaved, bay Quarter Horse who had to scurry to keep up since his legs were shorter. Bringing up the rear and prancing all the way was a tall, bright bay of some sort with four white feet.

When they approached a clearing, the woman on the Thoroughbred halted and turned to ask her companions a question.

"Would it be OK if you stay here and I go ahead for a while, and hand gallop him?" she asked. "He wants to run, and I'll be right back."

The other two women agreed, and the Thoroughbred, an ex-race horse, was off in a flash reminiscent of his days breaking out of a starting gate.

The two other horses were taken aback by his hasty exit. The Quarter Horse, who had many years of experience as a heeling horse in team-penning events, saw it as a cue. He took off after the Thoroughbred as fast as he could go a few seconds later.

That left the prancing bay, which suddenly was alone and scared without his companions. Since they'd both left him at a gallop, he felt danger must be near. He leaped towards their disappearing rumps as his equally frightened rider tried to turn him in a circle.

Michelle knew she'd fall off if she couldn't keep her horse, Stallone, under control. She pulled her reins and used her legs with all her might to keep him circling. At first the circles were big ones done at a gallop, but they got tighter and tighter as she regained control. Finally they were tight enough that Stallone stopped, flummoxed.

The Thoroughbred and the Quarter Horse had already trotted back by that time, but their riders were wide-eyed and looking at something on the ground.

"What's that?" they cried in unison, pointing to a bloody arm in the center of the sandy circle. It had been kicked up from its shallow grave by Stallone's thrashing hooves.

"Oh my God! It's an arm!" Michelle replied, startled.

The three women considered their options and headed back towards their stable at a trot.

When they reached a white telephone repair van parked at the end of the street where the stable was located, they dismounted and knocked on its side door. It was no secret the workers inside were not telephone repairmen, but FBI agents keeping tabs on the mafia in the area. Breathlessly the women told the two FBI agents inside the van what they had found.

"Can you lead me to it?" one of them asked as he removed his headphones, which he had been using to monitor some hidden microphones in the barn. Small TV monitors rimmed both sides of the interior of the van.

"Sure," Michelle said. "But what will you ride?"

"My bike. It's in the back," he said. "Give me a minute, and we'll go."

The three equestrians led the officer to the site at a trot, while he kept back a safe distance so the noise of his motorbike wouldn't scare their horses.

The arm was where they had left it. After a little digging with a small, collapsible shovel he'd brought strapped to his motorbike, the FBI agent unearthed some more body parts. Michelle thought she might be sick when his shovel uncovered a bloody but headless torso.

"We'll take it from here, ladies," he told them, and once again the women retraced their path.

That was the end of it until the 11 p.m. local news on TV. The lead story was that pieces of a body had been discovered in a sandy area near the Staten Island Expressway, and they might belong to the missing mafia king, Emilio Russo.

Of course it was the talk of the stables the next morning.

"You girls had some excitement on your ride yesterday, didn't you?" acknowledged Mike, the stable owner.

"I didn't even know Emilio Russo was missing," Michelle told Conor, a part-time stable worker who often rode Major, a Thoroughbred stabled there that was owned by Russo's son. "Who would kill him, chop him up, and bury him in the sand by the dump?"

"How will this affect Major?" Conor asked in his Irish brogue.

Each day the following week, Michelle read the local newspaper's account of the investigation with great interest.

One reporter said Russo's own son, Vito, was under suspicion. It seems there had been some problems between the father and son a few months ago. Emilio had reportedly chopped off the fingers of his son's left hand when Vito was caught stealing from the family's restaurant in Brooklyn.

Two days later, the newspaper ran a story saying forensics tests had found Russo did not die of a gunshot wound, which had been suspected. The cause of death was barbiturates and a paralytic anesthetic found in his system.

"Barbiturates and a paralytic anesthetic?" Michelle read aloud. *That sounds like what vets use to put down horses. Maybe some vet is the murderer!*

The FBI made the connection too. The following afternoon an agent was at the stable asking questions when Michelle arrived. Mike and Conor were both mucking stalls in the main barn.

When Michelle saw Conor about an hour later, he was upset over his grilling.

"There are things you don't know about me or about Major," he told her. "But I swear, I'm not a murderer or a horse thief."

Michelle wasn't sure what to think, but she trusted Conor because of his excellent rapport with Major. She'd long ago learned that people who were kind to animals were usually good people. "I do believe you, Conor," she told him. "If you see or hear anything that might help, call me or the cops right away."

Conor assured her he would, but added he didn't think the police would believe him.

That night, Michelle got a call from Conor around midnight. She bolted upright when she saw the caller ID. He was talking softly on a cell phone, and she had to listen carefully to catch each word.

"Michelle, I'm hiding in the hay loft. Mike is saddling Major up right now!" he whispered.

"Where do you think he's going?" she asked.

"I think he's headed to the Double D, and he's going to ship Major out of here," Conor whispered, referring to a Western stable a couple miles away. "I've been keeping track of all the equine truck runs to stables in this area by pretending I needed to ship a horse, and asking when they had a truck headed this way to save money. The Double D was getting a new reining horse shipped in sometime today by one of the bigger horse transport lines. They probably ran late with the traffic. When that horse gets off the truck, I bet Mike will load Major onto it, and he'll be gone!"

"I'll call the FBI," Michelle said. "The agent that went with us on the motorbike when we found the arm gave me his direct number."

"Good," Conor said. "Can I ride Stallone and follow Mike? I can't lose Major!"

"OK, but stay far enough behind him so he doesn't see you," Michelle warned. "You know how excited Stallone can get. And don't underestimate Mike. Remember, if he's doing this, he is likely a murderer, or at least an accomplice to some vet who murdered Russo. I'll meet you at the Double D."

About 15 minutes after Mike left on Major, Conor struck out on the same trail riding Stallone. A full harvest moon illuminated the trail as he trotted along. Stallone was excited, as always, but especially on edge due to the shadows, the strange sounds of the night, and the fact Conor was riding him and not Michelle. He pranced along and obviously wanted to gallop. Conor forced him to stay at a trot, however, as it was crucial he avoided detection.

Eventually they drew close to the Double D. It was a little closer to Staten Island's infamous landfill than their stable, and a stench hung in the air. Even at night, seagulls and other birds circled the area.

The only light was the moonlight and an outdoor electric light at the edge of the barn, but Conor could see a large horse van parked next to the barn. He rode Stallone into a stand of trees off the trail so he could watch while remaining hidden in the shadows.

There was no sign of Mike, Major, Michelle, or the FBI.

Conor wrote the horse van's license plate number on his sleeve with a marker he had forgotten was in his jacket pocket, and tried to be patient.

About 10 minutes later the big door to the main barn slid open, and a man Conor didn't recognize emerged with a black lead line in his right hand. He was still holding the lead line as he unfastened the latches of the horse trailer and let the back gate drop to the ground to serve as a ramp. He went into the trailer, and a few minutes later emerged with a Quarter Horse wearing a blanket, protective leg wraps and bell boots. Once the horse was off the ramp, two men came out of the barn and started to take the horse's leg wraps and bell boots off.

One of the men was Mike.

"OK; let me put this guy in a stall and then you can load your horse," the man working with Mike told him.

Conor wasn't sure what his next move should be.

A few minutes later, Mike approached the trailer ramp with Major, who took one look at the ramp, planted his feet firmly, and would not budge. His large head swiveled as he looked for Conor or Michelle for reassurance.

Stallone, sensing Major's fear, whinnied to him for comfort, exposing himself and his rider.

Mike moved toward the sound of the whinny, and Major moved with him. Within seconds, Mike spotted Conor and Stallone, pulled a black revolver out of his jacket pocket, and shot straight at Stallone's chest.

Luckily it was a moving target, and he missed. Mike was preparing to take another shot when Michelle jumped out of her parked car, which was hidden behind the barn, and tackled him. Her maternal instincts were on high alert, and she wasn't going to let anything happen to her horse. She landed a punch on Mike's jaw that was so strong it knocked him backward and also knocked out two of his teeth.

Major reared simultaneously. Mike dropped the lead line as blood spurted out of his month, and Conor charged onto the scene on Stallone. Major ran towards the other horse, as herd animals will do. That put Major's lead line close enough to Stallone for Conor to grab it, and then move a little to the left of the action.

When Conor looked back, he saw six FBI agents swarm around the horse van, their weapons drawn. Mike, the truck driver, and the Double D employee immediately put their hands over their heads. Michelle had taken a few steps backwards, and was pumping her arm in the air to check it for injuries after the force of her explosive punch.

One of the FBI agents told Mike he was being charged with grand theft of a horse and the murder of Emilio Russo, read him his rights, and hustled him off into a police car that had been hidden beside Michelle's.

"I didn't do anything!" Mike declared.

"Tell it to the judge," one of the FBI agents answered.

"Is everyone OK?" another of the FBI agents asked, and when they took stock, everyone was fine.

After that, it was a matter of simply winding things up.

"Do you want to pony Major back to our barn with Stallone, or should I ride with you?" Michelle asked Conor.

"It would be safer if we rode together," Conor told him. Michelle was still wearing the sweatpants and sweatshirt she'd worn to bed that night, a blue nylon jacket, and a pair of pull-on sneakers that had been beside her kitchen door, but she mounted Stallone. Conor borrowed a Western bridle with a simple snaffle bit from the Double D and got on Major bareback. Together they rode back towards their barn, after one of the FBI agents assured Michelle he'd return to the stable and take her back to her car, still parked at the Double D, afterwards.

"Do you want to fill me in on what your role was in this?" Michelle asked Conor as they moved along the trail.

"Yes, but maybe we should wait until tomorrow, so I don't have to tell you and the FBI the same story twice," Conor said. "Besides, I'm going to have a lot of work to do in the morning, since we'll be one person short for the feeding and the mucking out."

A companionable silence fell over them as they continued their way back through the moonlight. When they arrived at their stable, they untacked their horses and gave them a quick grooming. The FBI agent was there to take Michelle back to her car parked at the Double D. She arrived home at 4:30 a.m.

The following afternoon the two FBI agents who were the chief investigators in the case, Michelle, and Conor met in front of Major's stall. Conor dropped four bales of hay from the loft, and they sat on them to compare notes. Pal, the barn's border collie who had a habit of carrying stones in his mouth, dropped a stone in front of each person like a secretary distributing handouts in a conference room before a meeting.

The lead FBI agent started the debriefing lightly.

"We knew she had a horse named Stallone, but we didn't know she had a punch like Rocky," he teased Michelle. "It was a foolhardy move, but effective."

"Yes, where did that come from?" Conor asked.

"I don't know. I just wasn't going to let anyone hurt Stallone," she replied.

"I know how you feel," Conor said. "That's how I feel about Ashford, too."

"Ashford?" Michelle said, confused.

"Yes; let me explain," Conor began. "The horse you know as Major is actually a 5-year-old, Irish-bred Thoroughbred stallion named Kingdom of Ashford. He has never been raced, and he has no lip tattoo, but he comes from a long line of steeplechase champions. Even if he never competes in a race, he will always be valuable as a breeding stallion due to his excellent bloodlines.

"I used to work at the farm in Ireland where he was bred and foaled," he continued. "I was his primary groom and trainer. I was devastated when he was stolen from our yearling pastures one day in broad daylight.

"I was accused of the crime, I didn't have an alibi, and I panicked," he said. "I withdrew what money I had in the bank, left, and vowed I'd find Ashford, return him to the breeding farm, and clear my name.

"It hasn't been easy," Conor continued. "I have a strong suspicion about who stole Ashford originally, but I have no proof. I've been a step behind Ashford for several years, until I finally caught up with him here, in New York.

"I know Mike bought him at an auction near Saratoga," Conor went on. "He didn't know what he had, but he knew enough about confirmation he could tell Ashford was an excellent horse. I don't know why he put Emilio Russo's name on the bill of sale, but he did, and he had him shipped here to Staten Island."

"I can fill in that blank," one of the FBI agents said. "Mike owed Emilio at least $20,000 because Emilio had picked up some of Mike's gambling debts," he explained. "Apparently Mike had some 'sure things' at the track that ended up being not so sure. Emilio had a small string of horses in training at Aqueduct, and I bet Major was eventually going to join them, with forged papers.

"Mike knew Major had good confirmation, but he didn't know how good of a horse he was at first," the agent continued. "He signed the horse over to the Russos because he figured it was stolen property, and he didn't want to be charged with that. He didn't care if the Russos were though, and in a sense he was right because few people would mess with the mafia over a stolen horse."

"Mike didn't know Major's background?" Michelle asked. "I mean, Ashford's?"

"Not until recently," the agent answered. "We think he stumbled on an old ad the breeding farm ran in 'The Bloodhorse' offering a reward for Ashford's safe return, because we found a copy of that issue of the magazine in his tack box this morning. There was an ax with dried blood on it and a syringe wrapped in newspaper in the tack box too. They're already at the lab.

"We think he killed Emilio Russo for two reasons," the agent continued. "The first was the gambling debt. Then, when he found out how valuable Ashford was, he was selling him sight unseen for a lot of money to a big hunter-jumper barn in New England. We got that info this morning from the trucking company. Emilio wouldn't have taken kindly to one of his horses being sold without his knowledge. Mike was probably going to tell him some sort of big story and keep the money, but then decided killing him was easier."

"He killed Emilio Russo with drugs you would use to euthanize a horse?" Michelle asked.

"Yes; a track vet reported some of his drug supply was missing, and he had visited this barn last month to administer routine shots," one of the agents disclosed. "We believe Mike stole it from him. If the drugs could kill a 1,000-pound horse instantly, they could easily handle a 200-pound man. We don't know when or how he administered the drugs yet or why he cut the body up, but we hope to find out when we interrogate him in jail tomorrow."

"Does everyone think Mike acted alone?" Michelle asked.

"I do," Conor said, and the agents nodded affirmatively.

"I think his wife won't know any of this until we tell her that her husband is in jail," the second FBI agent said. "We never thought it was a mafia hit because too many things weren't their style," he continued. "The mafia would never have a body buried in the sand on a public trail. That didn't make sense."

"Other than Emilio, the only other person affected a lot by this was Vito Russo," the first FBI agent noted. "When I talked to him at his father's wake, he said he was done with horses, and he was going to stick with yachts from now on."

"Where does this leave you, Conor?" Michelle asked.

"This morning I called the owner of the breeding farm in Ireland who owns Ashford and told him I finally had him, and he was safe," Conor said. "He apologized for ever accusing me of anything, he offered me my old job back, and I accepted," he continued. "He has already faxed papers to the FBI to prove ownership. My first assignment is to oversee shipping Ashford back to Ireland by air as soon as possible."

"What about the people who originally stole Ashford?" Michelle asked.

"I've given the FBI my thoughts on that. They'll see if they can work with the Irish law enforcement to find any proof," Conor said. "It's been four long years being away from home for me, and I can't wait to return to Ireland.

"And Michelle, you and your husband have a standing invitation to visit us at the breeding farm in Ireland anytime," Conor said, "as do you two officers," he added, nodding to the FBI agents. "I will do a thorough evaluation of Ashford's current condition, and his owners and I will come up with a plan," he added. "I wouldn't be surprised to see him at the track or in the show ring before he goes to the breeding barn," he added.

The quartet looked at each other, sighed in unison, and looked at Ashford. Michelle slipped the horse a carrot between two horizontal boards of his stall, which he took without hesitation. The smell of fresh carrot juice fell over them as his teeth made crunching noises and the carrot disappeared.

11

Making History Come Alive

"We're going to Gettysburg? Wow!" Matt Thompson, age 9, jumped into the air in excitement when he heard the news. He gave his father and his mother bear hugs and even threw his arms around his 7-year-old sister, Jessica.

Matt's advanced social studies class had been studying the Civil War since school opened on September 8, a month ago. It was Matt's favorite class.

He was working on a paper about ex-slaves from Florida who served as spies for the Union Army. He found the subject fascinating, but there was little about it in either the school library or the library for the town of Melbourne, Florida, where he lived. This family trip, assisted in large part by the frequent-flyer miles his father accumulated from many trips to work overseas, would give him a decided edge towards an "A."

Matt's father was home from China for a week. They'd fly from

Melbourne to Harrisburg, Pennsylvania on Friday, spend two full days being tourists at Gettysburg, and fly home on Monday morning. Matt's mother had asked for permission from both of her children's teachers so Matt and Jess would have two days of excused absence from school. The request had been quickly granted due to the trip's educational value.

Friday's flights went off without a hitch, and they ended up with a plush rental car due to an unexpected upgrade. Many hotels were at capacity due to a popular apple festival in the area that weekend, but they stayed in a nice chain hotel a short drive away. It even accepted Matt's dad's points for an almost complimentary stay.

After a good night's sleep at the hotel, the following morning the family was among the first passengers on a double-decker tour bus's first run of the day around the Gettysburg Battlefield.

Matt was impressed with how big the battlefield was, how many monuments it had, and its many cannons. Although they'd been state-of-the-art when they were used and must have caused panic on sight, now the cannons stood silent, like any inanimate object whose time has passed.

Matt also marveled at the many old gray-wood, split-rail fences crisscrossing the fields like a child's set of Lincoln logs spread over carpeting in a family room. The fences still jutted across the now-silent battlefields, even though they'd been ineffective in keeping anything as major as a Civil War contained.

Matt had already learned about Pickett's Charge at school, but when he looked out over the rolling fields and imagined all the dying soldiers there, he grew quiet. He thought of the soldiers screaming in pain from their injuries. Others had whimpered as they lay on the ground, suddenly minus a leg or an arm. He knew many soldiers had been blown to pieces immediately, while others suffered for many hours, their blood spilling over the ground and making creeks run red as they lie dying.

He thought of the innocent horses that had died here too, obeying their riders to the end even though they had no idea what they were fighting for. Their instincts had been to run as far away from the area as possible, but their training forced them to suffer premature, violent deaths too.

Of course, sometimes brothers fought brothers during this horrible period in American history. The war had ripped families apart like it had ripped arms and legs off the soldiers who died here.

Matt knew some soldiers from Florida had fought for the North, while others remained Rebels until the end. The "Florida Brigade" of the South had fought in many battles led by Robert E. Lee, and it had charged Cemetery Ridge twice during the Battle of Gettysburg, including supporting Pickett's Charge.

"I'd like to find out more about the units from Florida in the war, especially the Union ones," Matt said to his dad after the bus tour. "Where can we go to find out about them?"

"Since it's supposed to rain this afternoon, I thought we'd spend the afternoon at the Gettysburg Museum and Visitor Center," his father, Brent, replied. "I think that would be a good place to start. I can already see there is way more to do here than we can cram into a long weekend."

After a light lunch, they watched a film at the visitor center and saw an amazing Cyclorama, a painting of the battle that was longer than a football field and four stories tall. They tackled the museum itself next.

After about an hour wandering through the exhibits, Matt hadn't found any information about the Union troops who were from Florida. His father suggested they ask a guide, who referred them to a "Resource Room" near the center's Education Center. Matt's mom and Jess were looking at other exhibits, but Matt's dad came with him.

A tiny man with wire glasses in the "Resource Room" came to their assistance.

"I'm sure we have some books that will help," he said. "If you give me a few minutes, I'll see what I can find."

Matt and his father sat in chairs next to a nearby table to wait. The man disappeared for a few minutes, and returned with several large volumes. He placed them on the table in front of them.

Matt looked through the first book, scanning the pictures. He did the same with the second book, and stopped suddenly at a reproduction of a daguerreotype on a page in the middle of the book. Its caption was simply "Members of the First Florida Cavalry Regiment." He couldn't be sure, but a young black soldier with a bamboo cane by his side looked familiar.

"Do you have a listing of all the members of the First Florida Cavalry Regiment?" Matt asked politely, trying to stay calm.

"I think there is one in the back of this book," the museum worker said. "Are you looking for a name in particular, perhaps an ancestor?"

"Something like that," Matt said.

The man moved the book so he could read it, rifled to a page at the back, and turned the book again so it was in front of Matt and his father.

"Here's a list of that regiment's members, in alphabetical order by last name," he said.

"It would be under 'J,' for Jefferson," Matt said, as his dad looked on, mystified.

Matt ran his finger down a long column of names, and stopped when he reached "Jefferson, J."

"There he is!" he said, excitedly. "The 'J' stands for Jonas."

"Let me see if I can find anything else on him," the researcher said, and once again disappeared.

"Matt, what is going on?" his dad asked. "Who was Jonas Jefferson?"

"Somebody I'm going to put in my paper," was all Matt would disclose.

Matt thumbed through the book with the photo and the list of names until the researcher reappeared with a smaller volume.

"Some of the members of that regiment attended a reunion here in Gettysburg 20 years after the battle," he said, pointing to the book. "A Jonas Jefferson is mentioned."

Once again, Matt did a double take. "Jonas Jefferson, an ex-slave, served the First Florida Cavalry Regiment with distinction as both a cavalry officer and an informer," he read aloud. "That means he was a spy, Dad!"

"Yes, it appears so," Brent said, still confused. "But who is he to you, Matt?" he pressed.

Matt's parents had raised him never to lie. He knew he wouldn't be believed if he said he'd met Jonas Jefferson in July while sitting on a bench at the beach in front of their home. If he told them he had played a little game with him called "What If?" to beat boredom and improve his imagination, they'd probably lock him up in a mental ward.

"I may have met one of his descendants once," he lied.

"May I have a photocopy of this page?" he asked the researcher. "I need it for a paper I'm writing for school."

"I can do that," the researcher said. "We're always pleased when young people take an interest in history."

"Wait!" Matt interrupted him as he was closing the book. "May I have a photocopy of the cover too?"

"OK," the researcher said, although he wondered why Matt was interested in a photo of a silver circle with two crossed swords in the center. "That's the standard insignia for a cavalry unit," he said.

"I meant the emblem below that," Matt said. "The one of the six-pointed star."

"That was the symbol of Florida during the Civil War," the researcher said.

"OK," Matt said, trying not to show his excitement. "Thank you for your help. It was great!"

By that time the rain had stopped. Brent and Matt found Jessica and her mother looking at a display of women's apparel of the day.

"I wouldn't have survived wearing all that tight underwear and those hoops, especially in the heat," Matt's mom, Liz, admitted.

Since they'd seen the major highlights of the visitor's center, they left, piled in the rental car, and returned to the battlefield to see it at a more casual pace than they'd done in the double-decker tour bus. They'd picked up a two-CD audio tour set, plus a map of the tour route, in the museum's gift shop. The map said the tour would take about four hours to complete. They'd see how far they got, and pick it up in the morning if they didn't complete it today.

The battlefield was beautiful after the October rain. Most of the trees had already turned color, although the peak of the fall foliage was still a week away. As Brent drove through the battlefield, stopping where instructed to by the tour narrator, the enormity of the battle and the suffering that occurred on these fields on several hot days in July 1863 hit home. The family learned more than 165,000 men fought at the Battle of Gettysburg, and nearly 51,000 of them were killed, wounded, captured or missing. It was the largest battle ever fought in North America.

Although Matt remained intrigued, everyone could tell Jessica needed a nap. They stopped around 5 p.m. and found a family restaurant for dinner. Matt and his parents were ready to call it a day, but the meal gave Jessica a second wind.

"Now what are we going to do?" she asked when they were back in the car. "Let's go see another movie!"

Since she'd been a good sport for most of the day, the family let her choose a movie. The latest animated Disney film at the mall had nothing to do with Gettysburg or history, but she enjoyed it.

It was well after 9 p.m. when the movie was over, so the family headed back on U.S. 30 towards their hotel. It wasn't raining, but fog was enveloping the area. Everyone except Brent, who was driving, was nodding off until he ran over a pipe in the middle of the road that had been dropped by a truck. The rental car's left-front tire went flat immediately.

Brent pulled off the road at a tiny rest area consisting of one picnic table and a green metal trash barrel. Rolling hills darkened to deep purple could be seen in the distance, surrounded by thin streaks of fog. Soon the only light they'd have would be from the traffic itself, which was intermittent due to the night and the weather.

"Oh boy," Brent said as he got out and surveyed the situation. "I can probably change the tire myself in the time it would take for the auto club or the rental car company to get here, if I have enough light to see."

He got to work. Liz stayed in the car, but Matt and Jess got out and sat at the picnic table to wait.

And that's when Matt noticed five riders on horseback cantering through the fields perpendicular to the road, slipping in and out of the fog. As they got closer, his eyes grew round when he saw most were dressed in the clothing of Civil War Union soldiers.

Leading the way was a black man wearing a straw hat and riding a black horse. He wasn't wearing a uniform, but had on dark clothing. His horse, which was at least 16 hands high, had a curb bit on its bridle, wore a martingale, and had a McClellan saddle. The man had a pistol and bullets in a leather holster around his waist. A rifle inserted into a scabbard was strapped to his saddle. A bamboo cane was also tied to the saddle, next to the rifle.

The riders were coming right towards the stranded car.

When they reached it, the lead rider pulled up, and the others followed suit.

"Good evening, Master Matthew," Jonas Jefferson said politely, looking at Matt. "All quiet tonight?"

Matt wondered why the men and the horses weren't wisps of vapor like he thought ghosts should be. Jonas Jefferson was so close and so real, Matt could even see the skin tags on his face and neck.

"Good evening, Mr. Jefferson," Matt replied.

Jessica could see the riders too, but they were invisible to Matt's father, who continued replacing the tire, or his mother, who was still dozing in the car's front seat.

"Hello, Miss Jessica," Mr. Jefferson added to Jess. "It's nice to see you both again."

"Looks like his horse threw a shoe," joked another one of the soldiers, nodding towards Matt's father before spitting a wad of chewing tobacco out of his mouth.

"It appears he's almost finished," Mr. Jefferson said. "It would cause havoc if we tried to help since he's too old to see us."

He didn't say anything else, but looked at the children through kind eyes. He moved his reins on his horse's neck, signaling it to turn.

The black horse arched his neck, pawed at the ground, and began to comply.

Matt had thousands of questions, but none of them would come out of his mouth. In the last few seconds, before the soldiers were gone, Matt blurted something out though.

"What if?" he said clearly, suddenly standing at attention and saluting Mr. Jefferson with his right hand. It was a question, but the way he said it made it also sound like a cheer.

"What if, indeed!" Mr. Jefferson replied, pausing to address him before cantering away. He returned Matt's salute, smiled, and disappeared into the fog settling further over the rolling hills of the Pennsylvania countryside.

12

The Case of
The Missing Toddler

Liz Thompson was cycling through the radio stations on her Porsche Cayenne's sound system as she headed back to her real-estate office in Melbourne, Florida, after a showing that November morning. She was about to push her thumb on the steering wheel control to move past a sportscaster lamenting the latest performances of the Tampa Bay Buccaneers when an amber alert interrupted the distressed sportscaster.

Liz, a mother herself, pushed the volume up on the radio and tried to ignore the buzz on her cell phone, which was signaling the same alert through social media.

The reporter gave the basics. "The missing child is a 21-month-old boy, with brown hair and brown eyes. He is 36 inches long and weighs 24 pounds. He was reported missing by his parents, a young couple living on the west side of Melbourne. He was wearing a white, short-sleeve T-shirt and red pajama bottoms with small blue dogs on it over his diaper. He was last seen in his crib set up on the first floor of his home. No other information is known, but if anyone spots the child, they are to call the police. He is considered to be in extreme danger."

Liz hoped she was wrong, but she had a sinking feeling she knew the family. A few months ago she'd sold a fixer-upper on the west side of Melbourne to a young couple that was relocating from New Jersey, and they had a toddler about that age. She called her assistant and asked for the mother's cell phone number.

Amy Brown, who was in her late twenties, answered her phone on the second ring. By the anxious tone of her 'Hello,' Liz's fears were confirmed.

They talked a few minutes, and Liz said she'd swing by their house. She knew the Browns had no family in the state, and they hadn't been in Florida long enough to have made many new friends.

When she pulled onto the long gravel driveway leading to the couple's small farm, there were already two mobile TV units setting up and about 20 police cars parked in various spots around the old, two-story house. One police officer stopped her, but let her continue when she told them she was a friend of the family and they knew she was coming.

She didn't have to knock on the door because it was already open. Amy and her husband, Rick, sat on a large, gray modular sofa in their living room, answering questions posed by an officer seated beside them. A crib placed behind a bay window at the front of the room was already enclosed in yellow crime-scene tape. Another officer was dusting the window and the crib for fingerprints.

Liz stood by the front door until Amy motioned for her to come closer.

"Thank you for coming, Liz," she said softly. "We're both scared."

"I'm sure they're doing everything they can," Liz said, trying to find some words of comfort.

"Terry was down for his nap; we set the crib up here in the living room, beside that window, while we're working on renovating the upstairs bedrooms," Amy said, pointing to the crib. "We don't have a baby monitor. We didn't hear anything, but we had the radio on while we stripped wallpaper upstairs," she continued. "I stayed with him until he went to sleep, and then went upstairs to continue to work. When I checked on him again about an hour later, he was gone, and one of the screens was up on the window."

Police officers, some with dogs, were already searching the grounds. As Liz looked out the window, she could see two men in scuba gear preparing to search a pond to the left of the property's small barn. They both had black wetsuits. One's air tank was bright yellow, and the other's was neon green, offering pops of happy colors despite their ominous assignment.

The officer who was quizzing Amy and Rick was thorough. He asked Liz for her contact information and her relationship to the couple too.

Another officer marched into the living room and addressed Amy and Rick. "Would you like to make a statement to the press?" he barked. "You can, or you don't have to; it's up to you."

Amy looked at Rick and Rick looked at Amy.

"Not now," Rick said with a catch in his throat. "Please tell everyone to look for our son. Share those photos of him that we gave you too, please."

"We have several task forces combing the grounds right now," the officer with the notebook said. Liz later learned he was Detective Jeff Heller, the lead investigator on the case.

"What can I do?" Liz asked.

"There's not much anyone can do except look for him," Amy said sadly. "He can only say a few words. He can walk, but he gets tired easily. He mostly crawls, and he crawls up on everything."

"Do you think he crawled out of his crib and got out of the house through a door or that window?" Liz suggested.

"I think anything is possible," Amy said, folding and unfolding her arms. "I know he can get out of his crib; I saw him doing it once before. We need to find him now; it's going to be dark soon."

Liz nodded. The bay window in front of the crib was open, and a light breeze was coming through it. She remembered from the listing that the house's air conditioning didn't work. It was one of many items the couple would have to have repaired or replaced in this fixer-upper.

She also remembered the screens in that particular bay window were old and flimsy. She had opened that window once herself when she was there for a showing. The screen had slid up on its own when she was preparing to raise it to let a fly escape.

She was about to mention that to Detective Heller when they all noticed the noise of a helicopter joining the search. It circled the farm methodically, rotating like the Earth moves around the sun.

"It looks like everyone is doing everything they can," Liz repeated. "You have to stay strong. Speaking of that, have you had any lunch? It's almost dinner time now."

"We haven't eaten anything," Rick replied. "I don't think we can eat."

"You need to try," Liz said. "I'll go to the convenience store a couple of miles down the road and get some sandwiches."

When Liz returned, she had sandwiches, soft drinks, macaroni salad, and potato chips for the couple, and plenty of extras for the officers too.

Amy didn't eat anything, but she appreciated having Liz to talk to.

"They didn't find anything in the pond," she said, bringing Liz up to date since her run for food. "I know an alligator that's about 8 feet long lives in it."

"Most alligators don't eat from November to March," replied Liz, a lifelong Floridian.

Amy looked at her, going over all the horrible possibilities in her head.

"I need to go now and pick up my own kids, but if you need me, call me on my cell phone, any time, day or night," Liz told the couple, handing each of them her business card.

"OK; thank you," Amy said.

Liz was troubled by the reports of the case on the 11 o'clock news on TV. Terry still hadn't been found, and the case was the lead story, of course. One reporter said the police were investigating the possibility the child was kidnapped with the intention of selling him for adoption or to child traffickers, but no ransom request had been received.

The reporter also mentioned the pond on the property, and the possibility Terry crawled towards it and was eaten by an alligator.

"Several alligators have been seen there, and it's still warm enough for alligators to be eating," the reporter said, discrediting what Liz had told Amy. "There have been cases where a human stepped on a submerged alligator and was eaten. There's also the possibility no alligator was involved, but he just drowned," the reporter continued.

That's great; I'm sure Amy and Rick are listening to this, Liz thought.

There was nothing new to report the following morning except a toll-free number had been set up for any possible tips. At noon the reporters showed several new groups of volunteers searching the area on foot, on horseback, and on all-terrain vehicles. A heartfelt video of

Amy and Rick imploring anyone who had any information to come forward, as well as thanking the police and the volunteers for their help, followed on the evening news. Photos of Terry accompanied all the reports, and soon were seen on flyers posted all around town.

Liz organized a search group made up of the employees of her real-estate office and their family and friends. The police instructed them to comb one section of a wooded area near the property. Three hours later they came up without Terry but with large welts from mosquito bites despite sprays, long sleeves and long pants.

Liz contacted two grocery store chains and the local restaurant association, and soon there was a steady supply of meals and bottled water being delivered to the Brown residence.

Amy did another video that ran everywhere on social media, pointing out every minute that elapsed without them finding her son made an unhappy ending more probable. It was impossible to watch it and not feel her angst.

The police continued to search and were checking every tip. The FBI was called in, but still there was no sign of little Terry Brown. Detectives and police officers conducted interviews of anyone who had been in the area, including the workers who were helping the Browns with their home renovation.

"It's a tough case," Detective Heller admitted to Liz on one of her visits. "We don't have any evidence to work with; he disappeared with no trace. We're following all the leads and all the possibilities we can think of, but so far we haven't come up with anything. It's like he just vanished."

On one morning visit, Liz happened to see the list Amy and Rick had prepared for the police of the companies and workers who had visited recently as part of their home-renovation work. It was handwritten on the top page of a yellow legal pad, with phone numbers accompanying most of the names.

As she looked at the list, a question came to Liz's mind.

"Amy, you said you were scraping wallpaper off the bedroom walls upstairs when Terry disappeared," she said. "But I noticed there is new wallpaper in the half bath downstairs. Did you have anyone wallpapering? I don't see a wallpaper contractor on this list."

"No, we decided to scrape the wallpaper ourselves before painting upstairs," Amy said. "I wallpapered that half bath myself because it was a small job. We had a quote for all the wallpaper work, but we thought it was a little high, and it was something Rick and I thought we could do ourselves to save money."

"Who did you have give a quote?" Liz asked, curious.

"A lady named Julie McCormack; she ran an ad in the shopper paper that gets delivered here free," Amy said.

Liz knew who Julie McCormack was. Julie had painted her laundry room a few years ago, but Liz didn't call her back to do any other work because something about her seemed a little off. She didn't have anything to go on except a feeling, so she didn't say anything more about it.

Back at work that afternoon, Liz searched through a box of business cards until she found Julie's card. Her address was in an apartment complex a few miles away, so on her way home she stopped by. She had to hurry because her kids would be getting home from school soon.

There was no answer when she rang Julie's doorbell at her front door, so she went to the back door to give it a try. There was no answer again. When she cupped her hands to peer through the glass of the door, however, she was surprised to see a high chair in the kitchen. As far as she knew, Julie was single and had no children.

"What are you doing?" said a cold voice behind her.

Liz turned around to find Julie. She had a toddler on her hip and a revolver in her hand that was pointed right at Liz.

"Get your hands up," Julie instructed.

Liz did as she was told. Julie bounced up two steps, unlocked the door with the gun still pointed at Liz, and motioned for Liz to go inside.

"Julie, that's Terry Brown, and you need to give him back," Liz told her.

"His name is Jimmy," Julie said. "Sit down on that chair," she added, pointing to a kitchen chair.

Although he wasn't even 2 years old yet, Terry knew what a gun was. "Bam! Bam!" he said, pointing his right index finger out like a gun and using his thumb like a trigger.

Don't encourage her, kid Liz thought.

Julie put the gun on the kitchen counter while she put Terry in the high chair, but once he was settled, she picked up the gun and pointed it at Liz again. Liz considered trying to tackle her, but there was never a good opportunity.

"Don't move a muscle," Julie warned her. She put the gun on the counter again, rummaged in a kitchen drawer, and pulled out several yards of yellow plastic rope, the kind often used in boating.

In a few minutes, she had Liz's hands and feet tied tight.

"Julie, stop now, before you get into any more trouble," Liz warned her.

"Shut up," Julie replied. She rummaged in the drawer again and pulled out a roll of silver duct tape. A minute later Julie had taped Liz's mouth shut. She picked up Terry and the gun again, walked out the door, turned and locked it, and disappeared.

Liz scanned the kitchen, trying to locate anything that would help her break the rope. She half hopped and half fell over to the gas stove, and after a few minutes, she was able to maneuver her tied hands together and turn on a burner. She moved her hands near the flame next. She got burned a little, but eventually she got the hang of it and some of the rope melted. Once a couple of strands were free, she was able to pull hard against the rest of it until her hands popped free.

She tore off the duct tape over her mouth and hopped over to a kitchen drawer where she found a knife, and soon her feet were free too. She turned on the faucet at the kitchen sink and ran some cold water over her burns. In a few minutes the water had taken some of the pain away. Then she popped open the refrigerator, found a gallon of milk, and poured it over her hands while she held them over the sink.

She had put her car keys in a small fanny pack that Julie hadn't even noticed. She knew she had no time to spare, so she dashed out of the apartment, got into her car, and tore out of the driveway.

Julie was long gone, of course. Liz didn't know which way she had gone, or even what she was driving.

She came to an intersection and chose the route towards the highway as she reached for her phone and dialed 9-1-1.

The dispatcher was professional. Within minutes a squad car screamed by Liz, its lights rotating and its siren blaring. Liz slowed, and finally took a deep breath. She pulled over to the side of the road and made another call. This one was to her neighbor, Marjorie, who promised to go over to her house, get her son and daughter, and take them to her house until she could get home.

Liz merged onto the road and continued towards the main highway. She hadn't gone far until traffic was backed up due to an accident. As she impatiently went by the accident scene at a crawl, she saw a white Ford Focus had crashed into a palm tree off a turn in the road. Its airbags had gone off, and an officer was holding a gun on the woman driver. The woman was Julie McCormack.

Liz stopped a little beyond the accident scene, parked along the side of the road, and ran over to the car.

"I'm Liz Thompson; I called part of this in," she breathlessly told the officer with the gun. "Is Terry OK?"

Terry was in a laundry basket in the back seat of the crashed vehicle. He was crying, but he seemed more frightened than hurt. Julie's face was bleeding, she looked dazed, and she had a leg injury, but the police slapped handcuffs on her before they even removed her from the front seat.

Another squad car arrived at breakneck speed and Detective Heller jumped out. He already seemed to know most of the story.

"Are you OK?" he asked Liz, noticing the burns on her hands.

"It's a long story, but yes, I'm OK," Liz told him.

"I think these two are too, but we have to take them to the hospital to be checked out," he said. "Would you like to call Amy and Rick, tell them we have Terry, and have them meet us at the hospital?"

"I'd love to," Liz said.

The emergency room workers put ointment on Liz's burns and were bandaging her hands when Amy and Rick arrived. They met in the waiting room a few minutes later, and together she and Detective Heller filled them in.

"I know you want to see Terry right away, but they're still examining him," Liz told them. "As far as I could tell, he was fine."

Forty-five minutes later the little family was reunited with tears of joy.

Julie had a broken leg, but she was read her rights and arrested before she even went into surgery.

The Browns went home through a side door. Detective Heller

gave interviews to the members of the press who were waiting outside the main hospital doors. Liz slipped away unnoticed and headed home to her own kids.

In subsequent days they learned Julie was more than a little mentally unbalanced. She had always wanted to be a mother, but she was turned down during more than one adoption attempt when she didn't pass mental competency tests.

When she met the Browns to give them her quote on the wallpaper job, she was immediately attracted to Terry. Her fingerprints weren't on the window because she never touched it. She had been careful to only touch the toddler when she picked him up, and not the crib. She had simply driven to the Browns' house, waited in her car behind some tall grass until she heard the radio playing upstairs, entered through the unlocked front door, and took the child while he was sleeping in his crib.

Terry emerged unscathed from the whole experience except for a little diaper rash.

Liz's burns healed, and she had a lot to tell her husband when she called him via Skype that night, as he was on a business trip overseas.

The jury was not lenient towards Julie, who won't be up for parole until she's elderly.

The Browns continued their renovation work with many more friends than they had when they started, and the police, the detectives, and the press were able to produce a happy ending in their reports.

The alligator still lives in the Brown family's pond. They're careful to leave him alone and watch him from a distance. They named him 'Spike,' and as far as they can tell the biggest thing he eats is the occasional muskrat.

13

A Sprint Car Thanksgiving

While he was incarcerated on drug charges, Bobby Gaines dreamed about what he'd do when he was finally off drugs and free, but he'd never imagined his journey would lead him here. Yet here he was, sitting in the conference room of a Fortune 500 company, high on the 40th floor of a sparkling, contemporary glass office building in Manhattan. He was wearing his new suit, and he was seated across from a man he hated.

Bobby was an ex-sprint car driver. He got into problems with the law while he was addicted to the pain medicine prescribed to treat the injuries he suffered in a career-ending crash. He had kicked the addiction, but he still struggled with the never-ending pain, which was a disease in itself.

For the last six months, he'd been working as the team manager of a new World of Outlaws team that Al Saunders, a Central Pennsylvania car dealer, was building to compete next season. One of Bobby's first assignments was to try to find sponsorship for the team. He'd made a presentation to the marketing committee of Wolf Oil in

August. Now, a little more than a month later, he was in New York to get the committee's decision.

He hadn't expected to see Jude Sanderson here too. They were the only ones in the conference room, and they both were just waiting for the marketing committee members to join them.

Bobby had seen Jude's handiwork before when he was still a driver. Jude considered himself to be a marketing expert, but in Bobby's previous encounters with him, he found him to be more of a lazy opportunist. Rather than do the hard work of developing programs that gave companies good value for their sponsorship, Jude spent most of his time trying to steal other teams' sponsors away.

No matter what the outcome of this meeting was going to be, Bobby didn't want Jude anywhere near him.

Of course, Jude oozed false friendship towards Bobby.

When Tom Coy, Wolf Oil's director of marketing, stuck his head into the conference room to tell them both it wouldn't be long before the members of the committee would join them, Bobby got up and followed him out the door.

"What's Jude Sanderson doing here?" he asked Tom.

"He made a presentation to us on behalf of one of his clients in August too," Tom told him. "He said he'd beat whatever offer you were making. I had to at least listen to him to be fair to the company."

"He's a leech," Bobby said between clenched teeth, as he tried in vain to follow his pain clinic's recommendations about deep breathing to lower stress. "I'd like to find out how he knew we were talking," he added.

Tom didn't respond. In the next minute, the other members of the marketing committee filed into the room, so they joined them and took their seats. Bobby sat as far away from Jude as possible.

They avoided eye contact, like two adversaries who already knew the other's best moves and were ready to counter them if necessary.

Tom addressed the group, thanking them all for coming.

"We had two interesting proposals this year from two sprint car teams that want to join our motorsports program, which as you know already includes an Indy car, a sports car, and a drag racing component," Tom said. "We've been thinking about including a sprint car program for some time, and we feel the timing is right now to do so."

Well, that's good to hear, Bobby thought.

"Both of the proposals we considered were strong, but we decided to go with the one presented on behalf of Al Saunders Racing," he said.

Bobby breathed a sigh of relief, and a wide smile spread across his face.

Jude wasn't going to give up easily, however.

"I'm sorry I have to bring this up, but you should know that Bobby here is not someone you should be associating with," Jude told the group, right in front of Bobby. "He's a convicted felon, who did time for drugs.

"I don't know what he told Old Man Saunders to get his job, but he's not a stable person," Jude went on. "You'd be far better off to go with my team, which has no such dirty laundry. You'd be jeopardizing Wolf Oil's reputation and turning off a lot of fans if you went with his team."

Bobby's eyes widened, but he remained quiet. Part of what Jude said was true. He had done time, but he'd been honest about it. If Jude was going to change the committee members' minds now, when he was so close to a deal, it would be the last straw.

It was so quiet in the room that its occupants could hear only two things: the wall clock ticking, and a fire truck on the street 40 floors below.

Luckily Tom was undeterred.

"We've made our decision, and we're committed to it," he told Jude, rising from his chair. "We thank you for your presentation, and you can feel free to contact us in the future with other opportunities. Now, we need to go over the details with Bobby."

Jude gave Bobby a look that could kill, got up, and left.

"Now that he's gone, we can tell you even more good news," Tom told Bobby. "We're glad you were honest about your past and told us about your accident, your drug addiction, your incarceration, and your struggle to manage your pain. We feel your story can be inspirational to both young people and to others who have to deal with pain daily. That's why we're prepared to double the amount of money you asked for to expand the program into outreach to schools and hospitals, so you and your driver can tell people what you've learned, and give them hope to do the same. We're getting that part of the budget from the Wolf Oil Foundation, not the marketing budget."

Bobby looked at Tom and then at each member of the committee. All were smiling. Bobby couldn't stop the tears that sprang into his eyes. He wiped them away as he tried to regain his composure.

"I can't tell you how happy I am, and how thankful I am for your decision," he told them. "I haven't had much to be happy about for a long time. We'll be glad to include a program for schools and hospitals next year."

"This isn't just a one-year deal, Bobby," Tom continued, smiling also. "We've prepared the contract for a three-year deal, with an option to continue for another two years after that. You need to look it over, and then both you and Al can sign it, have it notarized, and return it to us and we'll be able to make the announcement to the press. Have you made a decision on who the driver will be?"

"We haven't approached him yet, but with your approval, we'd like to sign Kevin Whitaker," Bobby said. "He's young, talented, and good with the press and the fans. He has been doing a lot with a limited budget, and he deserves a break."

"We thought you deserved a break too, Bobby," Tom said.

"I can't thank you enough," Bobby repeated, as the other members of the marketing committee broke out in applause. "I think great things are ahead for all of us!"

Bobby thought about calling Al as soon as the meeting was over, but he waited until he was at work the following day so he could tell him all about it in person. Al was delighted, of course. The paperwork was signed, and Al gave Bobby the go-ahead to call Kevin Whitaker and offer him the ride. Kevin's reaction was over the moon as well, especially since his current car owner had told him he couldn't race next year due to a downturn in his business.

There was much to do in the following weeks and months. Bobby and Kevin spent two solid weeks at Wolf Oil's corporate headquarters and a regional plant to learn more about the company's history and its business. Kevin spent a third week back in Manhattan undergoing some press training. There were renderings and graphics to approve, as well as some more equipment to buy and some more employees to hire. Bobby also was the liaison between Wolf Oil and Gary Griffith's trucking company, as Gary had promised to start using Wolf Oil products in his large fleet of trucks as a business-to-business component of the sponsorship.

While he was working with the graphics company, Bobby solved the mystery of the leak to Jude Sanderson. Although Bobby had a non-disclosure contract with them, Jude used the same graphics company, and most likely saw a rendering of the Saunders car with its proposed Wolf Oil livery that was on an easel in the company's studio during one of his visits. After Bobby explained his theory to the company president, new policies were put into place there so that would never happen again.

The drawings of the car and its transporter advertising Wolf Oil were approved, and the wraps were installed. The team had enough money to start the season with seven cars and eight engines. Al Saunders Racing already had a beautiful transporter complete with Lista cabinets too. The team would debut at the Performance Racing Industry show in Indianapolis in December. Its first race of the season would be in February in Florida, after some private testing in the same state in January.

Bobby still struggled with constant pain, but he was learning how to handle it better. He was happier than he'd been since his accident, and he accepted a friend's invitation to Thanksgiving dinner.

Emily worked full-time as a dental hygienist and part-time in timing and scoring at a Pennsylvania track. She'd been supportive throughout his ordeals, and happy he had found a way to stay active in the sport. Bobby was glad he wouldn't be alone for the holiday. Besides, it was more convenient to stay in Pennsylvania than fly to Boston with his mother for Thanksgiving at his brother's house.

Bobby fit in with the crowd assembled for Thanksgiving at Emily's parents' house. He learned although most of the people there were Emily's relatives, others were family friends and neighbors. It seemed the door was open to all.

Over 40 people were seated at four different tables throughout the house for the traditional turkey dinner with all the fixings. Another group ate at the picnic table in the home's sunporch. A few of the kids ate seated on the stairs to the second floor, balancing their plates on the steps above them. Luckily it was a clear, crisp fall day, and a few guests ate on the home's wide front porch.

Bobby and Emily ended up at a card table in the living room, right in front of the fireplace and a big-screen TV that was transitioning from the Macy's parade to football.

One of Emily's brothers and his wife joined them. The brother was a Kevin Whitaker fan, so the conversation was lively. The atmosphere was festive and the food was delicious.

Never one to hide what she was thinking, Emily got into a friendly battle with Bobby over whose football team was superior. It was never settled, but later they both enjoyed watching an impromptu game of touch football that broke out on the front lawn by those who weren't sleeping off their turkey dinners.

As Bobby looked at the contented family gathering, he wondered how he and Emily had ever become friends, since they'd never even been alone.

Although Bobby was not unscathed, he was grateful he had made it through a difficult period of his life. He was also never as thankful for his many blessings, and never more excited for the future.

About the Author

Fall signals the start of school. Many of us have photos of the first day of school at different ages, or the obligatory elementary school headshots. Here's Linda Mansfield's school photo from fourth grade. She was 9. She hadn't gotten braces yet, but she already loved to read.

Linda Mansfield is an award-winning reporter, editor, author, and public relations representative. She is a former editor at a Manhattan publishing house. She was the first female editorial staff member of "National Speed Sport News," and her work appears regularly in its successor, "Speed Sport Magazine." She owns Restart Communications, a public relations agency based in Indianapolis, Indiana, in the United States.

Her first collection of fictional short stories, "Stories for the 12 Days of Christmas," was published in 2015. In 2017 she released three sequels: "Twelve Stories for Spring," "Twelve Stories for Summer" and "Twelve Stories for Fall." Although the reader's experience is enhanced if each book is read in order, they can also be read separately. There are no cliffhangers or "to be continued" lines.

Authors need reviews so readers discover their books. If you liked "Twelve Stories for Fall," Mansfield will be grateful if you'd leave a positive review on the Web site of the outlet where you purchased it.

Authors also need to build e-mail lists of people who might like to purchase a new release, and to prove to publishers they have a following. To join Mansfield's e-mail list, please fill out the form on her Web site at LindaMansfieldBooks.com. Her e-mail list won't be sold, and readers can unsubscribe anytime. Those who sign up will receive a free short story as her thank you.

Readers can also follow Mansfield on Facebook at "Linda Mansfield — Author," on Twitter at @RestartLMAuthor, and through her blog at LindaMansfieldsBlog.wordpress.com.

Don't miss the other books in the "Two Good Feet" series!

1

2

3

4

WITHDRAWAL

CPSIA information can be obtained
at www.ICGtesting.com
Printed in the USA
LVOW11s2107081217
559123LV00008B/673/P